OUR HOUSE
ON THE HILL

BY

NYDA A. WRIGHTSMAN

PublishAmerica
Baltimore

ISBN: 1-60813-151-3
PUBLISHED BY PUBLISHAMERICA, LLLP
www.publishamerica.com
Baltimore

Printed in the United States of America

Chapter 1

Elkton was a popular resort town during the early part of the nineteenth century. The town's people liked to brag about how royalty and presidents had stayed at the Elkton Hotel. It was a popular vacation destination for the rich and famous; although in recent years it had lost most of its charm, and of course with this depression had very few guests at all. The railroad ran right through the middle of town, therefore travelers had easy access to the hotel. The railroad was about the only mode of transportation until automobiles became available. After that the fortunes of the town took a downturn. By the mid thirties Elkton had lost a lot of its magnetism.

The depression was hard on everyone in the small town. It was especially hard on the Jackson family. Life was good for the little family until the crash of nineteen twenty nine. Harry Jackson had been working on the railroad for a few years and life was looking good. Then the depression hit. Harry lost his job and there was no work to be found. They had four children to feed and Alice was pregnant again.

Having no job, and with no promise of one, Harry would hang around Charlie's garage to see if by chance he could find an odd job. Sometimes he was able to make a dollar or so. He could do almost anything, and was a willing worker. The garage did not have a lot of business these days. There were not very many people traveling through town any more. Several of the fellows would just stand around gossiping about hard times and how they hoped that soon something would break. But every day seemed to be worse than the one before. Try as they might it seemed that the little town of Elkton was dying.

When the eviction notice came, Harry was not at all surprised. He had rented from the Harrison family for a couple of years, and up until the last few months they were doing fine. But these last six months he had fallen behind. The Harrison's had really been very nice about it. They had let it slide for several months, and Harry had seen this coming. He couldn't blame them. They needed money too. They had two boys in high school. So the Jackson's were forced to move from their rented home, and there was no place to go. Alice spent many nights walking the floor and crying with her infant son Harry. Soon they would have another child, and how were they to feed any of them? Christmas was couple of months away. They had no place to live and they must move within the next few weeks. Where to? What then?

It happened one day while Harry was hanging around just praying for anything that would get him some kind of work, a man came puffing into the garage. He was soaked with sweat and panting so hard he could hardly get a breath between words.

"Oh Lordy," he said "I've walked all the way from the ball field. Blasted car stopped on me at the ball field and won't take another step." Charlie came out from the back room, where he had been eating his lunch, and said "Well, hello there, Joe. It sure is good to see you again. What are you doin' in this part of the country? I thought you had moved to Washington DC."

"Well, I did, but you know I had Old Jake taking care of the place for me and he just up and died, and I need to decide what to do with the place. I hate to sell her, and if I did my wife would divorce me. She was born in that place and she said she hopes she can die there. Personally, I think it is more bother than it is worth especially with the housing market being on a down hill slump. Living so far away, we don't even get to come up much any more. In winter the weather is too bad, and during the summer we just don't have time to do what we want to do".

Joe Kinney owned one of the grandest places in town. It was a beautiful place about two miles out of town. Joe and his wife had lived there for about six years after their marriage. After Marge's mother had died and Joe was elected to congress they had moved to Washington. Jack Montague, whom everyone called "Jake", had been living in the house for a few years, as care taker. He had recently been found dead by a neighbor. Therefore Joe was left without a caretaker.

"Do you think you can come out to the ball field with me and see if you can figure out what is the matter with the car?"

"Sure," said Charlie. Then turning to Harry said "Harry, I will probably need some help, I don't know too much about these contraptions either. If you don't mind why don't you come along with us? We will see what we can do. Here Joe" he said, handing Joe a cold drink. "You need a cold sarsaparilla, and you need to rest a bit. Just sit there a spell, and we will be ready in about ten minutes." Then, going to the foot of the stairs he called for his wife Lois. They lived in a small apartment above the garage. "Honey," he yelled. "I have to leave for awhile. You will need to come down and watch the shop."

While Joe rested, Charlie and Harry started gathering up what tools they thought they may need and putting them in Charlie's old truck. "Boy," Charlie said, "Talk about luck. I knew about old Jake dying. I hadn't thought about that place. But it might just be a streak of luck for you."

"What do you mean?" asked Harry.

"Joe's place," said Charlie "don't you see? Joe needs a care taker. That is a perfect job for you. Think about it."

"But I have four kids and the fifth on the way. Joe wouldn't want five kids living in that mansion of his. Jake was an old man. He didn't have a family. He was perfect."

"No" said Charlie, "Not really, he couldn't do repairs and such.

When the place needed the roof patched or something like that, Jake had to call someone like you to do it. You could do it yourself."

"That's true, but I still don't think Joe would hire me with five kids. I guess it wouldn't hurt to ask though, because with Christmas coming, and also a new baby at about the same time, and not even a place to hang my hat, it sure can't hurt."

"I agree completely. You are in a really bad predicament that's for sure", replied Charlie with a chuckle. "I wouldn't want to be in your shoes. I wish you luck though."

"Come on Joe" Charlie said. "Let's get going"

As the three men crawled into the truck Joe said, "I don't know why I didn't just take the train. I should have known something like this would happen. Seems like I traveled better on old Bessie, all I had to do was feed her and she took me where I wanted to go. Of course I don't even have old Bessie with me any more. And she was a lot slower; I was hoping to save time. Anyone with an ounce of sense should know these cars are just for show. They look nice, but they sure will never be as reliable as old Bessie."

The other two men laughed uproariously. "You sure got that right. It seems like someone is always bringing one of those things for me to fix. But maybe they will improve them in a few years. Sure would be nice. They travel much faster than old Bessie" said Charlie.

"I'll tell you boys" said Harry, "I would give my eye teeth to own one. But I would never buy anything on credit, and with five kids I'm sure I will have to just continue wishing. I just hope I can find some way to keep bread on the table and a roof over my head."

"By the way, Joe" Charlie said. "If you are looking for a new caretaker here's your man. Harry here is in need of a job and a place to live, and you would look a long time for someone better suited for the job. He can do nearly anything and a more honest man you will never find."

"Harry would you be interested in the job?" Joe asked turning to look at Harry.

8

Harry replied, "sure I would be interested, but Joe you know I have a family. I have four kids and another one on the way. We are expecting our fifth around Christmas."

"Well son that is a big place in the country. It would be a great place to raise kids."

"Oh I know that, Joe, but I just thought that maybe you wouldn't want kids there. As for the work, Charlie is right. I can fix just about anything. And I am not afraid of work."

"This job doesn't pay enough to keep a family that size. I gave Jake free rent and a small allowance, but I couldn't pay big money. I'm really sorry about that."

Harry's heart started to race. If Joe had no objections to kids, maybe they could work out something. At least Alice could sleep at night if they had a roof over their head. He had heard her walking the floor and crying, and it broke his heart. Now maybe he could do something about it.

"I'll tell you what" Harry said to Joe. "Why don't you come to the house for dinner tomorrow evening. I can talk with my wife tonight and maybe we can come up with a solution to both our problems."

"Well I never turn down a free meal. And it would be great to get rid of this headache I've had for a couple of weeks. There's my car." Joe said, just as they turned the curve.

Jumping from the truck Joe got the crank from his car, and cranked it up. The car sputtered, and seemed to choke, then simply died. "Crank her up again" said Charlie as he opened the hood and looked at the engine. Joe did so, and again the car seemed to clatter, and choke, then stopped abruptly. Harry stood watching and listening. Several times the car started, stammered and then quit. After listening for a few minutes Harry said "I think I found the problem. I think the timing might be off. Hold on a minute." Reaching into his pocket, he pulled out a small gadget, and working diligently for what seemed like only a few seconds, raised his head from under the hood and said, "Now try her again.

Joe turned the crank and the car started to purr like a kitten.

After paying Charlie what he asked for the trip out there, Joe reached into his pocket and pulled out a five dollar bill. He handed it to Harry.

"You were right, you can fix just about anything" said Joe.

That was the most money Harry had seen for weeks. "You don't owe me anything" Harry said. "I just came along for the ride."

"And you fixed the problem in a shake of a lamb's tail. Take it. It was well worth it to me. Thanks Harry. And if you meant it about the invite, I would love to take you up on that dinner if you are sure your wife wouldn't mind."

"I'm sure she wouldn't mind." Come on over around seven," said Harry. "We'll see you then."

"I'll be there with bells on" said Joe as he jumped into his car and drove off.

Charlie and Harry got into the truck and headed back towards town.

"Well Harry, maybe this is your lucky day" said Charlie, "I think you made an impression on Joe".

"That may be so, but I'm sure it will take a lot to convince my wife that this is luck. I know exactly what she will say. She will never consent to take this job and move our kids into that house. I just know she won't. Alice worries about everything. And I am not sure that I want to consider this myself. I am not afraid of work, but I would not want to take a chance on my kids ruining something out there."

"I think you worry too much too. If Joe needs a man, and you are a man, that sounds like a real winning situation all around. Don't turn it down too soon. You need to give it a chance I'm sure it will work."

On his way home that evening Harry stopped at the grocery store and bought the largest cracked knuckle he could find, it still had a little meat on it. He knew that Alice could make some great vegetable soup. They had planted a big garden and luckily Alice had canned a lot of vegetables. He hoped she wouldn't be upset that he had invited a stranger to dinner when they were so near broke.

Harry was so excited when he got home. He was pleased that he had some good news for a change. He told Alice about what had happened that afternoon and gave her what was left of the money after spending some for the soup bone. Alice was elated when he told her that he may have a place to move the family. But after he told her the whole story about the proposition, she was not at all happy. She thought it would be wonderful if it could be true. She had been so worried, and she felt sure that Harry would come up with something. He had always taken care of them, and she should have known he would move heaven and earth for her and the children. But she still knew that this was out of the question

"Oh Harry" she said when he explained it all to her. "Don't be so ridiculous. Our five kids in that mansion? You must have been out of your mind to even suggest such a thing. It's out of the question."

Why in the world would this man allow them to move into his wonderful mansion with five children? And if he did, wouldn't she worry herself to death wondering if one of her children might do something to damage some of its majestic hardwood floors, or some kind of artwork or fancy walls. There were also those beautiful gardens and people said the lawn was like a velvet carpet. How could she be sure that her kids wouldn't ruin something? She had tried to teach them good manners, but this would be asking a lot from them, as well as herself. She really wasn't sure at all about this. Alice had never actually seen the house. It was rather secluded out there behind the trees. She had heard people talk about it though and she knew that it must be like a palace from the way people talked.

After putting the children to bed that night, she told Harry about her fears. "As much as I would love for this to happen, I am just afraid it would never work. I don't think you know what we would be expecting from our kids. They are good kids, but they are kids. They have to be allowed to be kids. That is a mansion out there on that hill. Children have no idea about how easily some of that stuff could be damaged."

"Don't worry about all that right now, honey" said Harry. "This guy seemed to think it might work, He even told me that he thought it was a wonderful place to raise a family. Maybe we can work out something. That was the reason I asked him to dinner. We will just lay it all on the table, and we won't make our decision until after we have thought about it carefully. But as I was talking to that guy this afternoon, I felt like God had shown me the answer to our prayers, I'm hoping I am right."

Lying in her husband's arms that night Alice felt that maybe this was an answer to their prayers. She said a little prayer, and asked God to show them the way. She fell into a sound sleep, and slept all night. It was the first full night's sleep she had for weeks.

When she woke the next morning, Alice felt completely rested. It was a crisp day in early October and she could still hear the birds chirping outside her window. She hurried to the kitchen and built a fire in the kitchen stove before the children woke. It was getting chilly these fall mornings. She put on the coffeepot and the kettle. She would cook breakfast before waking Irene. She heard little footsteps on the stairs. Jean was already coming downstairs. The others would be down shortly.

Alice found herself humming as she dished up oatmeal for her children. She had to rush Irene through her breakfast. Irene sometimes dawdled in the mornings. She loved school, but sometimes she would rather stay home and play with the other girls. After Alice got Irene off to school she fed the baby, and diapered him. Then she put him in the crib in the living room. The other children, Audrey and Jean always entertained the baby while Alice cleared the breakfast table and washed the dishes. After that she would dress the girls and send them outside to play. Harry had put a gate on the porch outside the kitchen, so that Alice could see them from the kitchen window.

After the children were out to play, she and Harry sat and had breakfast. Since Harry had not been working they had gotten used to taking that extra little time in the morning to have a second cup of coffee, and just relax. They both hoped that, even though they enjoyed this time together, it would not become a habit. He really needed to find some sort of a job.

Harry left to go back up to Charlie's. Maybe he could get another lucky break. As he went out the door Alice said "Grab a dime from the sugar bowl up there and bring home a box of crackers. I know you and the kids would rather have rolls, but most people like crackers with soup, and since we are to have important company this evening I think we can splurge. I want everything to be as nice as I can make it, no matter how this turns out". She set out to making the soup for supper.

By the time Irene got home from school that afternoon, Alice had baked a batch of bread, saving enough dough for a pan of rolls. She had a large pot of soup simmering on the stove, made a beautiful apple pie and had straightened the house. She looked around their little home and felt satisfied. Their furniture was all hand-me-downs. Harry's sister had given them her old furniture when she had gotten new. It didn't really look bad, except for Harry's chair. While he was working on the railroad he would sometimes come home dirty and tired. He would fall asleep in that chair before changing. Alice had covered it with a nice quilt and it looked rather nice now.

While Harry was at Charlie's that morning, Mrs. Clary came running into the garage at about eleven thirty. She said "Can anybody here help me? My cow is trying to have her calf, and I am afraid she is dying. I can't seem to do anything for her. Henry is out of town and he won't be home until late this evening".

"What seems to be the problem?" asked Mr. Griffin who was just sitting there chewing his tobacco.

"I don't know," said Mrs. Clary. "I think it is trying to come feet first. I have no idea what to do".

"I don't either" said Mr. Griffin. "I guess you will just have to leave her alone and hope she does. Most times animals know what to do. Best thing to do is let nature take its course. ".

"I can't do that" said Mrs. Clary. "I can't just watch and listen as the old cow dies. I have been up all night with her.

I don't know what to do either' said Harry, "but I'll bet my wife would. She was raised on a farm, and she knows a lot about animals I will run down and ask her if she knows of anything we can do".

Harry ran down and asked Alice if she knew what to do with a cow that was having a calf feet first".

Alice said "One time I remember that daddy had an old horse that was having a colt like that. He pushed the colt back and turned it around somehow, but I wouldn't be able to do that. I don't know what to tell you"

"Do you think I could save the old cow if I did that?"

"I have no idea, but she will definitely die if someone can't do something"

Harry ran back up to the garage and Mrs. Clary had already gone back to her barn. Harry ran to her barn and told Mrs. Clary what Alice had told him must be done.

"Will you help me"? She asked Harry.

"Let's see what we can do" Harry said. Rolling up his sleeves Harry went to work. They worked for over an hour trying to get that calf. Finally they did get the calf. He was dead, but as soon as the calf was born, the cow seemed to find some strength.

"I believe your cow will be alright. I'm sorry about the calf though. I think maybe if we had been sooner, we might have saved it."

"At least we were able to save the cow. I was hoping for heifer calf anyway. Really didn't want a bull." said Mrs. Clary. "Thank you so much for your help"

She gave Harry fifty cents. Harry went home and told Alice that they had lost the calf, but that he thought they had saved the cow and that Mrs. Clary had given him fifty cents for helping her. Now Harry needed to clean up before going to get the crackers for dinner. He cleaned up and changed his clothes. Then he went to the store for crackers. He came back at about four thirty.

Alice panned the rolls and set them to rise. She wanted them to be fresh and hot when she put them on the table for dinner.

Harry was beginning to feel that maybe things were looking up some. He had made five dollars and a half in two days. It was not a lot, but better than the last few weeks. The only thing he needed now was a job with some security. They didn't know where the next dollar would come from and still they were not sure if they would even have a roof over their head for the coming winter. Alice called the girls from outside and got them ready for dinner. "We are having company for dinner girls, and I want you to be good little girls during dinner. After we finish eating I want you to go to your room. Irene you can play with Audrey and Jean for a little while then I will come up and tuck you in. Can you do that for me dear? "Yes Mommy but what if Audrey won't listen to me. She never wants to listen to me," said Audrey.

"She is always so bossy," said Audrey. "Why does she have to be so bossy?"

"Girls" Alice said. "Nobody has to be bossy. Please don't start that squabbling again."

"Girls", said Harry. "When I was at the store today, Mr. Walters gave me a nickels worth of candy. After we finish eating, you may have a piece of candy if you will be good girls while Mommy and I have company."

Mr. Walters, the grocer often gave a penny's worth of candy to children when they came into the store. But Harry's children seldom went to the store, so he would often give Harry a nickel's worth to bring home to them.

"Oh Daddy", said Irene "do you have a tootsie roll. I love tootsie rolls."

"Yes you can each have a tootsie roll after dinner." With that the girls all danced with glee.

There was a knock on the door, and Harry shushed the girls and went to answer it.

"You're right on time Joe." Harry said. "Come on in".

Harry introduced Joe to Alice and the children.

"I hope you like vegetable soup," said Alice.

"It is one of my favorites, and I could smell it before you opened the door. It smells delicious," replied Joe.

When Alice took the rolls from the oven, and the aroma wafted through the kitchen, Joe remarked "Oh it smells like I have died and gone to heaven. Nothing smells better than fresh bread coming from the oven."

Laughingly Harry pulled out a chair and said, "Well, just sit down here and we will see if it tastes as good as it smells."

During dinner they talked about the weather, and the depression, which was on everyone's mind nowadays. Joe was running for his third term in congress, so naturally the conversation turned to politics. Both men, being republicans, soon turned the subject to Franklin Roosevelt who was running for President. There was no debate. They both agreed that it was time for a change, but neither believed that FDR was the answer.

At one time during dinner Irene asked "What is an economy crisis Daddy?"

Joe laughed, "I think we have a bright little girl here. How old are you little girl?"

"I'm nine, and my name is Irene" replied Irene, "and I heard Mr. Carr talking to my teacher today, and he said something about an economy crisis. Now you and Daddy are talking about it too, and it sounds like something bad."

"Well honey," Joe replied "it does seem to be something pretty bad. But I hope you never need to worry about it. It is hard to explain to a little girl. It means that for a couple of years now, people have had a hard time finding work, and that people don't have much money. Grownups are trying to fix it so that little girls like you will not have to worry about it."

Turning to Harry he said, "I think we are worrying your children with this line of conversation. I think we should change the subject…"

"I think so too", said Alice. "Is anyone interested in a piece of apple pie?"

After dessert, Joe pushed back his chair and announced, "That was a delightful meal Mrs. Jackson. Thanks so much for inviting me. I seldom get a home cooked meal when I am traveling, and I really enjoyed it."

"You are welcome. It wasn't much but at least it was filling. And call me Alice. I feel like an old woman when people call me Mrs. Jackson."

"Harry, take Mr. Kinney into the living room and I will bring you both a cup of coffee as soon as I can make a fresh pot. It is a little more comfortable in there."

Chapter 2

Harry and Joe retired to the living room and Alice proceeded to clear the dishes. She put on a fresh pot of coffee to perk. Deciding to leave the dishes in the sink for awhile, she gave the girls their Tootsie rolls and sent them upstairs.

Alice didn't want her husband or their visitor to know how nervous she was. She didn't know whether she wanted to even consider what they were proposing. In one way, she wished so much that it would work out. Their situation, as it was, had to change. But was this the answer? On one hand, it would put a roof over their heads. And it was a beautiful roof at that. She dreamed of living in that great big elaborate mansion. She would feel like a queen. But she worried about the children. Would she be able to let them play like children, or would she have to cage them up to keep them from damaging some complicated piece of art, or keep them from destroying some elaborate flower bed? Her children meant the world to her, and Harry just didn't understand what a handful they were sometimes.

"Well here goes", she thought, as she filled cups with coffee and put them on a tray with sugar and cream.

Harry and Joe had been carrying on a conversation in the living room while Alice cleared the dishes and took care of the children.

"That little girl of yours is a smart little thing. Who would have thought she was even listening to our conversation?" Joe said as they sat down.

"Yes, she never misses a beat" Harry answered. "Sometimes I think she is too old for her years."

"Well, let's get down to business", said Joe. "Did you speak to your wife about our conversation yesterday?"

"We talked a little last night, but Alice isn't comfortable with moving into that house with the children."

"Let's see what we can come up with." Joe says, "What I am concerned about is that I can't afford to pay you what I know you would be worth. As I told you, I gave Jake a small allowance, and free rent, but it was in no way enough for a family. You would have to have something to supplement it."

"I will be completely honest with you, Joe" said Harry. "I have been picking up odd jobs for several months now. My wife is a very frugal woman. She raised a lot of vegetables in her little garden this summer, and canned a lot. Then sometimes she makes a dress for one of the neighbors. She is really good seamstress. She makes a little now and then. We have been keeping afloat, but I got behind on my rent, and I am being evicted from this house. We have to move by the last of October, and we have no place to go. I thought your deal sounded good with just the free rent. But I am afraid I jumped the gun a little. Alice says she doesn't think we should take the offer, even if it does sound like a gift from heaven, because of the kids."

Just then Alice entered the room with a tray. "Here's fresh coffee. I will need to go up in a little while to tuck the girls in, but they will be okay for a little while".

Joe said "Thank you. We have been talking about the proposition I offered Harry yesterday. We are both hoping that we can convince you to accept the offer. Here's what I propose. I don't know if you have ever been in the house, and if you wish, I can take you out there tomorrow and you can see it for yourself. The house was built with servant's quarters at the back. There are six rooms at the back of the house, with a back stairway leading to the upper floors. If you are concerned about the children, they would not even have to enter the front at all. That would be the best solution. As for the gardens and the yard, of course the children would be welcome to play there. With moderate care I am sure they would not damage anything, and if they pick a posy now and then for their Mommy, I think that would be nice. I remember picking flowers for my mother. I could offer you free rent and two dollars a week. But I was thinking last night though, that if we could make this a family affair, it would be even better. If you could keep the place clean, just keep it dusted and the things women need to do. Wash the windows now and then and things like that. We would not have to send a crew in when we are ready to come home for a weekend, or when we want to entertain a few guests. When Jake was there that was what we had to do, and it was a real problem sometimes. If we could count on you for that we could double that. Does that sound doable?"

"I have no problem with work. I do have four children, and soon I will have five. They are my first priority. They are the first thing I think of in the morning, and the last thing I think of at night... The reason I am concerned is that they are just small children. They do not understand the value a dollar. I am sure that some of the things in that house are priceless. I would not want to be responsible for my children breaking or ruining something important."

"To begin with" said Joe "we do have some priceless art work. It is not in that house. Those things were moved with us when we went to Washington. I'm not saying that nothing in the house is of any value What I am saying that with moderate care nothing would be damaged so badly that it could not be fixed. And I understand that your husband can fix nearly anything, and if he can't, I'll bet you could do a pretty good job. I heard how you helped save Mrs. Clary's cow this morning, and you weren't even there".

Alice laughed.

"I'll tell you what" she said. "Let's go out there tomorrow. We can ask Mabel to take care of the kids for an hour or so, and we can go out and take a look. I don't want to promise anything. I want to be sure before we can give you an answer."

"Okay, but why not take the girls too. I'm sure they would enjoy being out in the country for a few hours. It is a nice place for kids."

"I think not this time. I think it would be better to leave them with Mabel. They love their Aunt Mabel and she likes spending time with them."

"If you think that is best. But you are welcome to take them" said Joe.

"Let's just do it this way. I would rather not worry with the girls tomorrow anyway. That way I can concentrate better. But right now I need to go up and tuck them in. It is their bedtime. Irene has school tomorrow.."

"And I must go. Thank you for having me to dinner. I really did enjoy it. May I pick you folks up in the morning at around ten?"

"That will be fine. But you needn't rush off; I just need to tend to the children. You men may visit as long as you wish" said Alice.

"No, thank you" said Joe. I must be getting back home. Goodnight. I will see you folks in the morning…"

After Joe had gone Alice said, "Honey, will you run up while I put the kids to bed and ask Mabel if she has time to watch the kids tomorrow morning. I don't think we will be gone longer than an hour or so. But I would rather not take them with us. I would just feel better going without them".

"Okay" said Harry, "whatever you think dear".

Harry's sister Mabel lived up the street a few blocks. She often took care of one or more of the girls when Alice was busy. Her children were grown, and she enjoyed having the little ones around. Actually, she had practically adopted Audrey. The little girl would have stayed with Mabel if her mother would have allowed it. And Mabel loved allowing her to spend the night at least once or twice a month. She tried not to show favoritism, but it was hard. Audrey had Aunt Mabel wrapped around her little fingers.

Mabel's husband Ed was the company doctor in the town of

21

Linwood about twenty miles from Elkton. He had a home there and commuted on weekends. But he was the only doctor in both towns and made trips back and forth as needed. He had delivered all of Alice's children, and would deliver the next one in a couple of months.

When Harry reached Mabel's he asked his sister if she would take care of the children tomorrow while he and Alice went with Joe to his house.

She said "you know I will. Maybe we can bake some cookies tomorrow. We haven't done that for some time. They love to help me cook".

Joe has asked me if Alice and I would like to take Jakes place as caretaker out there" Harry said.

"That would be a great job for you, if it pays anything at all" said Mabel.

"Not much" said Harry "but rent is included. That accounts for a lot in my eyes."

"Yes I'm sure it does, but it would be better if it would pay a decent living wage"

"Well I am afraid Alice doesn't think we should take it anyway" he said. "She is afraid that the kids might ruin something. I think she is much more worried about that than even Joe. He seems to think we could handle the job and the kids. I think so too, but you know Alice".

"Well" Mabel said. I hope it works out for you. I will say a prayer for you tonight".

Mabel and her husband did as much as they could to help Harry and Alice. Since Harry had been out of work, life was pretty rough for them and Mabel knew it. She hoped that this might be a turning point for the little family.

The next morning after Alice had fed the children breakfast, she helped Irene to get ready for school. Then she dressed the other children and took them up the street to their Aunt Mabel. Mabel was waiting on the porch for the children. She was a slightly overweight older woman with hair as white as snow. She had a smile as bright as a summer day, and it was easy to see that she loved these children as much as if they were her own. Mabel had two cats Midnight and Whitie. They were both sitting on Mabel's lap as she sat on the old swing.

"Good morning" Mabel greeted the children as they came up the steps." I am so glad to see you. How would you like to help me make some cookies today?" She lifted the cats off her lap, and put them down, taking the baby from Alice. "Oh yes, Aunt Mabel" Audrey said. "You know how I like to make cookies."

"Me too" said Jean. "I want to help too. Aunt Mabel, Can I help too?"

"Sure", said Mabel, "You can both help. As soon as little Harry goes down for his morning nap, we will make cookies. Do you want to make chocolate or peanut butter?"

"Chocolate" said Jean. "Peanut butter" said Audrey.

"Wow" said Alice "I think you have just created a problem for yourself. It is usually better not to give them a choice. They never agree on anything."

"That's alright" said Mabel. "We will figure it out. You run along. We will fight it out."

"Well, good luck" said Alice. "We won't be too long this morning. I am afraid this is just a waste of time anyway. Harry thinks this can happen, but I have very strong doubts."

"Don't turn it down too soon" said Mabel. "You might be able to work out something. I wish you luck."

"Thanks, I will need a little more than luck I think." And with that she turned and left the porch. The children waved goodbye, as their mother went down the street toward home. Alice hurried home and she and Harry got ready to go.

Mabel took the children inside. She sat the baby on the floor to play. She went to the kitchen and came back beating on a lid from an old pan with a wooden spoon… "Here you go. You can make the music while your sisters and I make the cookies" she said.

NYDA A. WRIGHTSMAN

While Harry contentedly pounded on his 'drum' Mabel and the girls went to the kitchen. Aunt Mabel handed the flour to Audrey and the sugar to Jean. "Here" she said. "Put these on the table. I will get the butter, eggs and milk". Mabel gathered all the ingredients and set them on the table with the sugar and flour. The girls pulled out a chair and stood on the chair on either side of Mabel. They knew what to do. They did this often. They loved helping Aunt Mabel make cookies. As Mabel put flour in the measuring cup, she allowed Audrey to scrape the excess flour from the cup with a knife. Then Jean did the same with the sugar.

"We're getting good at this aren't we" said Aunt Mabel.

"Yes we are" said the girls in unison.

Mabel measured butter, and sugar into a large bowl, and creamed them together. Then she set out two small bowls and handed each of the girls an egg. Without being told what to do, each girl broke her egg into a small bowl and as Mabel held out the larger bowl, each girl poured her egg into the creamed mixture.

When Little Harry started to fuss, Mabel covered the cookie dough with a clean tea towel and left it on the table while they went to tend the baby. Mabel gave him a glass of milk then she changed him and laid him on the couch. He put his thumb in his mouth. He was soon asleep. They went back to the kitchen. Mabel helped the girls to wash their hands, and after washing her own, they returned to their task.

After the dough was mixed, Mabel put the wad of dough out on the counter. The girls helped to flatten it out. Then Mabel gave the rolling pin to Audrey. She rolled for awhile, and then Jean took her turn. When it was just about the right thickness Mabel took a turn. Aunt Mabel gave each of the girls a cookie cutter. Jean had a dog and Audrey a sheep. Mabel helped them to cut out the cookies, and place them on the cookie sheet. She sprinkled them with sugar. And put them into the oven. Then they watched the clock. When the cookies were done, Aunt Mabel took them out of the oven and put them on a rack to cool. They then cut out some cows and some horses. They made four sheets of cookies. Aunt Mabel gave them each half of a peanut butter sandwich, and two cookies with milk for their lunch.

Meanwhile, Alice and Harry sat on the front porch waiting for Joe to come in his car to pick them up.

"Harry, do you really think we should even consider this? I have a feeling it is just an impossible dream" said Alice.

"Don't be so pessimistic dear. Joe seems to think it will work out. It is his house. Maybe when we see what he has in mind for us, we will decide that at least we can give it a try. Besides that, snow will be falling soon and if this doesn't work the only other thing I can think of, is that we would have to beg Mom and Dad, or Mabel and Ed to take us in. You know how I would hate that. I am sure one of them would take us in, because of the kids. But God, Alice, I don't know how I bring myself to start begging."

"I know honey, and I promise to keep an open mind. You know it is the children I am concerned about."

Just then Joe pulled to the curb in his automobile. As they got into the car Alice said "Are you sure this is safe? I have never been in a car before. How fast does it go?"

Well, I have had her up to twenty five miles an hour and she rides rather smooth on a smooth road. But on a rocky road you get a pretty rough ride."

Chapter 3

Joe drove down the road and every time he turned a curve Alice held on to Harry's hand like she was afraid she would be thrown out. Harry could see that she was very nervous and tried to sooth her. She had always been a very excitable person and panicked easily. Harry wanted to laugh, but Alice also had quite a temper, and if he laughed, she would probably make them stop and let her out. Joe had a big smile on his face and Harry quietly hoped that Joe wouldn't say anything to upset Alice. She was nervous enough that if she got angry, there would be hell to pay. He kept talking to Joe to keep him from noticing how upset Alice was. He just hoped that by the time they got there, Alice would be calmed down. As the house came into view, Alice forgot how scared and nervous she was.

"Oh" she said. "Is that the house? That is the most beautiful house I ever saw. It does look like a palace."

The first thing Alice noticed was the round tower on the left side of the building. It was fanciful, almost flamboyant, covered with cedar shingles. The house was a Victorian style house built in the Gothic Style. It had pointed gables, tall chimneys and a towering spire. It looked like an old castle from the middle ages. The top of the tower looked almost like a steeple. There was a wrap around porch that went around two sides of the building with a second story porch on one side. There were large groupings of windows. The landscape was in harmony with the house, making it look like a painting. It was spectacular. Alice was in awe.

"Oh", she said. "No wonder people talk so much about this place. But I know now that this is impossible. Our kids are growing like weeds, and I would worry myself sick if they were in that house, even if we owned the place. And we don't. I think we should just turn around and go back to town."

"Whoa" said Joe. "You haven't even seen the place yet. Just wait until I show you the rest of the house before run away." Driving around to the back of the house, he pulled up next to a much smaller porch. "Now you can get out, and we will go in at this end."

As Joe unlocked the door, Alice thought "there is no way we can take this job. Why doesn't Harry see that?"

As they entered the house from the back she saw that this end of the house was not nearly as elegant as the front. There was a kitchen nicer than the one in which they were now living, but not nearly as splendid as what they had seen thus far, There were two doors on her left as she went in the door. One door led to a walk-in pantry. The other led to a laundry room. To her right was a living room, modest, but very nice. Leading from the living room were two other doors.

"I want to show you this part of the house first", said Joe "because I don't want you to run away yet." He opened one of the doors which led to a circular staircase leading to the second floor. Upstairs were two bedrooms. One was smaller than the other. "I think this was once a nursery" Joe said "and it could be one again. And there are two more bedrooms just like these on the upper floor." He said as he led them up another flight of stairs.

Coming back down to the second floor, Joe said, "This door in the master bedroom, leads to the front hallway. But we will go through the parlor this time," leading them back down the stairs.

This time he opened the door to the front of the house. It was like walking into another world. Alice had never even dreamed of such splendor. They stepped into a room which Joe called the library. There was one wall almost completely lined with books. The furniture was mostly hand made, and all varnished in the same color as the woodwork. The windows were lined with beautiful draperies. There was a gorgeous chandelier with gas lights.

From the library they entered into the tower. The round room had a beautiful grouping of windows, draped the same as the library, and lavish furnishings. The gas lights in this room were on the wall. Alice could imagine how beautiful this would be at night with these lights turned on. Each room they entered took her breath away. Just outside the round room was a foyer. To the left, there was a beautiful wide circular staircase leading to the second floor. To the right was a door opening onto the front of that beautiful wrap around porch.

There was a formal dining room, and a beautiful kitchen with a butler's pantry and scullery. From the kitchen there was a door leading to the back side of the wrap around porch. Joe opened the door and they stepped onto the porch. "The porch furniture is stored right now in a room in the barn" said Joe. "We store it in winter. We usually spend a few weeks here around Christmas, but no one needs to sit out here in the winter weather. Storing it for winter was also easier for Jake."

As they walked up the circular staircase, they saw a balcony all around, from which there were six bedrooms. One of them was the master bedroom in the servant's quarters. There were six bathrooms in the house.

The round room had a round handmade bed with matching bureau, and chifarobe. "This is one of several guest rooms on this floor" said Joe. From the hallway, Joe opened one of the doors, to show them that it opened into the master bedroom, which they had seen earlier at the back of the house. .

The third floor was almost identical to the second, having two less bedrooms allowing for the upstairs porch.

Alice stood in amazement as she looked at first one room and then the other. How could anyone who owned a beautiful house like this, move out and allow strangers to live in it.

After the tour of the house, Joe took them to the barn. He showed Harry to the tack room, saying "We only have one horse at the present time. She is my wife's pet. She is too old to sell, and Marge would not hear of getting rid of her. Since Jake died, Tom Smith has been keeping her for me at his place. Part of your job of course, would be to take care of her, feed her and exercise her now and then. She is very gentle, Alice. I am sure you and the children will love her. Do you ride?"

"I used to ride some" said Alice "I was raised on a farm over on the mountain. I love animals."

"Maybe. come spring, you can teach the children to ride too."

"Well I'm still not so sure about that."

They walked through the barn and Alice thought "I would be happy living in this barn. It is nicer than most of the places I have lived." But she kept that thought to herself. After seeing the house and barn they strolled all the way around the house, looking at the grounds, and landscape. Everything was spectacular. Alice allowed herself to dream, at least for a little while. Finally it came time to go back to town.

Harry looked at his watch and said "My goodness, it's nearly two thirty. We better go get our children before they drive Mabel crazy."

Alice said "When I left they were deciding if they would bake chocolate or peanut butter cookies. I could see that Mabel was going to have a fight on her hands. I hope Mabel won."

"If I know Mabel we will have two kinds of cookies when we get there."

Chapter 4

When the three of them climbed into the car, Joe said "I won't ask you for a decision right now. I can give you a day or two. I want the two of you to talk it over. Tom will keep the horse for a week or so longer. I spoke to Larry Haynes yesterday, and he said that he might be able to take care of the place until spring if you decide to turn me down. But when spring comes he has too much to do on the farm, so I will have to find someone before then. I am hoping that you folks will decide to accept my proposal. I will try though not to pressure you."

Harry asked Joe to let him and Alice out of the car at Mabel's house so they could get the children. The kids were glad to see their parents, but the girls did not want to go home.

"We made cookies, Mommy. Aunt Mabel said we can bake peanut butter ones next time we come to visit her. Can we come tomorrow?"

Alice looked at Harry and smiled. She knew he was thinking, "Mabel won after all."

"I doubt it will be that soon "said Alice. "But from the looks of the size of that box of cookies, you won't need more of them for a few days at least"…

"Little Harry is napping" said Mabel" I put him down a couple of hours ago so he should wake soon. Let's have a cup of coffee, and a couple of these cookies and you can tell me about your day."

Harry said, "Mabel, you wouldn't believe that house. It is really almost like a mansion."

Alice said "I was flabbergasted the whole time. I don't even know what he talked about. I was so impressed with the beauty of that place."

"Well" said Mabel, "are you going to take the job?"

"We have to discuss it some more" said Alice. "I still have some misgivings."

"Well", said Harry, "I don't see how we can turn it down. Under the circumstances, I think it is about the only thing we can do. We have to make the decision soon. Joe is in a hurry to get back home and we only have ten days before we have to move somewhere. A lot of men are out of work now, and I am sure that after word gets around, Joe will have no problem finding someone for the job. But if I don't take this job, I have no other prospects. I have been out of work for months, and Mabel, you know that without the help of Mom and Dad, and you and Ed, my kids would be going hungry" said Harry.

"Ed and I talked last evening." Mabel said "You know if you do have to move, and don't have a place to go, you could move in here with us for a few months if need be."

"Thanks Mabel" Harry said "but I hope it doesn't come to that. Not that I don't appreciate it, but I want to be able to care for my family and so far I have not been very successful. That is the main reason I want to do this."

When the baby woke, Alice gathered the children and saying their goodbyes took them and went home.

It was a long night for Alice. On one hand she was excited about the prospect of a job. She knew Harry had tried, but these last few months had been very distressing. Most days she was so depressed it was hard to get out of bed. Sometimes she just wished she could lie down and sleep forever. Then she would look into the face of one of her children, and she became ashamed of her thoughts. They needed her. Being needed kept her going when times were rough.

When Joe got back home that evening he felt reasonably sure that he had convinced Alice and Harry to take the position. He had at least one thing on his side. He knew that they were almost desperate for a place to live. He knew why they hesitated, but he was desperate too. If he left his house empty, it was hard to say what vandals and even the weather could do to it before his return. The insurance company would also cancel his policy if the house was not occupied.

Joe called his wife, Marge that evening. He told her about Harry and Alice and that he was really looking forward to getting them settled so that he could come home. Marge said that she thought it would be nice to have a real family living there. That was a perfect place for a family.

Alice and Harry talked well into the night and finally Alice told him, "Let's sleep on it. I will pray for an answer, and in the morning I will give you my answer."

That night Alice dreamed she was a princess, living in a great castle. It was a beautiful dream. When she awoke she felt like something good was about to happen. She did not remember what the dream was about, but she took it as a sign that they should not turn down this offer. She woke Harry and told him that she would start packing in the morning. Harry was elated.

Early the next morning Harry walked out to Joe's place to give him the news. Both men were happy with their decision.

Joe walked through the house again with Harry. Harry asked a few questions. Joe made a few suggestions. "The main thing for us right now is that someone is living in the house. The insurance will not cover it if there is no one living here. I don't think anything will happen, but you never know when lightening will strike, or the wind may blow something away. And with no one living here vandals could break in and destroy everything. Insurance companies will not cover uninhabited homes. That is one of the main reasons that we want the place occupied as soon as possible".

True to her word, after getting Irene off to school, Alice dressed the other children and fed them. She told them that they would be moving in a few days, and she started packing up their few belongings.

As the day wore on, Alice seemed to forget about the premonition she had the night before. She never told Harry about the dream because she really couldn't remember it. Soon it was forgotten as she packed their meager belongings and prepared to move her little family to the country.

When nightfall came, Alice was more tired than she had been in a long time. She hadn't realized how tiring this kind of work could be. When Harry came in, she told him "I hope we don't have to do this often. I am so tired I think I could sleep for a week. She fell into bed that night exhausted. She slept like she had not slept for a long time.

When Alice got out of bed the next morning, it was raining. It seemed that it was raining bucketsful. That meant that the children were inside all day underfoot. "What are you doing Mommy" asked Audrey. "Why are you putting all my clothes in that box?"

"I told you darling" said her mother. "We are going to move to a great big beautiful house in the country."

"But Mama" said Jean "I don't want to move away from here. I like my bed, and I want to play with my dolly."

"Of course you do, dear, and we will take your bed and your dolly with us. You will still be able to play with them."

All day the children were asking questions and Alice nearly lost patience with them. "Is Daddy going too?" "Will we still see Aunt Mabel?" "Can Irene still go to school?" "Why are we moving Mama?"

Harry spent the morning at Charlie's and then, decided that since no one seemed to have any odd jobs that day, he should just go home and see if he could help Alice with the packing. Alice was glad to see him. She said "The kids are about to drive me crazy. I wish you would help me to explain to them what it means to be moving. They seem to think it is a world changing event. I can't believe two small children can ask so many questions. I am nearly ready to shake the shoes off both of them."

Harry grabbed up both children, one under each arm, and sat down in a chair with one little girl on each knee. The girls giggled with glee. He said "Well Mom, it is an earth changing event. We are going to start a whole new life." Then to the children he said "And you two are going to be a big part of it. We are moving to a big house in the country. You will have a big yard to play in and there is a small room in the barn where we could have a cute little play house. There is a horse and we can have a dog. We can even have a few chickens if I can find enough money to buy them. Then we can have eggs for breakfast most mornings. How would you like that?"

Both girls seemed excited about the whole thing. Then Harry said "Now why don't you run up to your room, and tell your dolly all about it, and give Mama some time to do what she needs to do."

As the girls trotted up the steps Alice said, "Try to be a little quiet. The baby is sleeping. To Harry she said "You are so good with them. It seems like you never run out of patience."

"Just a nice guy I guess" He said. Then reached over and kissed her.

Alice and Harry worked well into the night preparing for the move. By the time they were ready for bed, everything was all packed except for things needed for dressing the children and breakfast in the morning. They fell exhausted into bed.

Moving day came and Harry's nephew Ted and his brother Earl were there bright and early to help him. He had borrowed a truck from Charlie, and expected to have their furnishings all moved early today. It still looked a lot like rain so Harry hurriedly piled their meager belongings onto the truck. It was only about two miles, so he thought that if he hurried they could still get there without getting everything wet.

After the truck was loaded the three men jumped in and headed for the new place. Alice would take the children to Mabel's, and wait until Harry came back to help her with them. She bundled up the children, putting on several layers of clothing because it was damp and chilly. When they got there, Mabel said "I am dying to see that place anyway.

Let's pile the kids in to my car, and go out and help Harry and the guys."

"Are you sure you want to do that? It looks like it might rain" said Alice.

"I don't think so" said Mabel "I think it is clearing up. I have a pot of beef stew, and some pickles I brought from the basement. We will take a loaf of bread and we can all have lunch. I'm sure the guys will be hungry after loading and unloading that stuff. The kids will have to be fed, and I am sure you have better things to do than to worry about cooking food today anyway."

"Mabel I don't know what we would do without you." Alice said as she hugged her sister-in-law.

The two women packed the four children in the back seat. Alice held the pot of stew and Mabel drove out to the Kinney place. When they got there the men were taking the last of the things off the truck. Alice took the children indoors. She sat the children down and explained that they were never to open the door to the front of the house. She told them that someone else lived in that part of the house, and whether the people were at home or not, the children were not to go in there. She told them that she and Daddy would be going in there from time to time, but that they were never to go there. Alice hoped that they understood. It was the one thing she worried about the most.

After the men had placed the furniture where Alice wanted it, they decided it was time to take a break and have a cup of coffee. Alice told the children they could go outdoors and play. She told them not to pick any flowers, and to stay near the house where she could see them. Then she took Mabel on a tour of the house. It was amazing that even the second time she saw it, she was still so enamored by it. She didn't think she could ever believe that people really did live in this kind of a house.

"As soon as I can get my own place in some order, I plan to clean this part of the house thoroughly. Once it has a good once over, it won't be hard to keep it that way. Now where the children are, that will be a different story".

After Mabel had seen the front of the house they came back to Alice's kitchen. They heated the stew, and called the children inside. They all sat down and ate lunch. Joe came in when they were just about finished eating lunch.

He said "I just stopped over to say I am leaving. I need to get back to DC. Marge hates it when I come up here without her. I guess if nothing happens we will probably see you again around Christmas time. I hope you like living here. If you have any questions or problems, you have my number.

"Would you like some lunch before you go?" asked Alice.

"No thanks" I just ate a few minutes ago. I need to get going. It will be late when I get home as it is.

Mabel, Ted, and Earl then left to go back to town. Harry returned Charlie's truck. When he returned he and Alice began putting the house in order. The first few weeks were very busy for Harry and Alice. Winter was setting in, and the old man who had been caring for the place had not really been able to do a lot. They set about winterizing everything they could. They were determined to do their best at this job. It didn't pay very well, but they had a roof over their heads, and hopefully they would be able to keep food on the table. The children followed Harry around a lot while he was working outside the house but he didn't mind. They were not allowed to go into the front of the house. Every now and then he would give them little chores, and they loved thinking they were helping. Some days it was too cold for them to be outdoors all day so they helped their mother indoors. Alice didn't have quite the patience that Harry had with the children, but she also had them for many more hours at a time.

Chapter 5

The next few weeks were busy for both Alice and Harry. As soon as Alice had their belongings in place, and their part of the house in order, she started to tackle the front of the house.

Alice was afraid of storms. She panicked during any storm, and especially if the wind was blowing hard. The children hated for it to storm when their father was not at home. If he was there, he could calm their mother down some, but the children just seemed to upset her more. There was nothing they could do right during a storm.

To know Alice was to love her. But to love her during a storm was not easy. She was beyond fearful, she was terrified, and she frightened anyone who was around her. Everybody who knew Alice knew this and even neighbors would try to rescue the children if they knew there was a storm brewing. She would take the kids and go to the cellar at the first sign of a storm and she would cry constantly.

The children learned at a very early age to remain as quiet as possible. Their mother could cry, and she always did, but if they cried she panicked even more.

Three days after they moved into the big house, there was a storm. It was just a regular autumn storm. There was thunder and lightening all around. Alice had taken the kids to the cellar. She had them sitting under a table. They were all quietly crying.

It just happened that Harry came home in the middle of the storm. He found the house empty, and immediately knew that Alice would have the kids in the basement.

When Harry found them all huddled under the table crying, he was angry with Alice. It was no use to try to change Alice. He knew that. But he knew that he could not allow her to keep frightening the children like this. He told Alice that she could stay in the basement, but that he and the children were going to go to the kitchen and get something to eat. She protested of course. She was afraid for her children.

Alice and Harry argued more when it stormed than they ever did about anything else. He took the children to the kitchen and soon the storm was over. After the storm, when he had her calmed down he talked to her about how she was making the children into a fanatic like herself. He said that fear was one thing, panic was another.

After the storm was over Alice when came up from the cellar she told Harry "I don't know why I do that. I know that I am frightening my children to death. I have tried, but when I hear that first clap of thunder, I go nuts. I think you understand what I am going through but the kids don't understand. I feel so bad for them. Oh Harry what can we do?"

"We have to talk about this Alice. I think you are getting worse. I can't stop the storms. And I realize I can't change you. So I have to find a plan. I am going to call the kids in from outside, and we are going to make a plan".

"I don't know what you are talking about"

"You say you know what you should do in a storm, but you can't do it, right?"

"Yes, I know I should not panic, but I do, and then I can't think at all"

This is what I plan to do. I am going to tell the kids what I want them to do when it storms. Then you are going to tell them that is what you want them to do also. I will send the kids to the laundry room, and you can go to the basement"

"And how do you plan to get me to do what you say when you are not here"

"Watch me" Harry said.

Harry called the girls from outside. He said "Girls we have something important we want to talk to you about."

"Did we do something wrong daddy?" Irene said

"No girls" Alice said. "I did"

Harry said "Jean what do you think when it starts to storm?"

"I'm scared" she said.

"But what are you scared of?"

"Mama gets scared, and the thunder is so loud"

"Do you know the thunder can't hurt you?"

"Yes, Mama told us that"

"Then why are you afraid of it"

"Because Mama gets scared" she said.

"See Alice, they are scared because Mama is"

"I know that dear. I just don't know what I can do about it".

"Irene, do you know what you should do when it storms?"

"I know we should come inside and don't play with metal and don't stand in front of a window"

"Where did you learn that?"

"Mama told us"

"And what does Mama do when it storms?"

"She runs to the basement and screams".

"Do you see what Daddy is getting at?" said Alice.

"Yes Mama you go crazy when it storms. We all know that"

Harry said "Are you willing to try to help us with that?"

"What can I do daddy?"

"Here is my plan. It is very simple. The next time it storms, you will help the other kids to come inside and to go to the laundry room Your Mama will go to the basement.".

"But what if Mama makes us go to the basement" she said.

"This is the important part. You will try to quietly remind your Mama about the plan. I am not giving you permission to disobey your mother. I am giving you permission to help her to remember our plan".

Alice said "There is one thing that I worry about. When I can't see the kids I worry about them. Won't this make me more frantic".

"I am hoping it will help you to come to your senses. If this doesn't help we will have to try something else. We have got to find something to help you. I believe that just maybe with a gentle reminder from the kids, you just may lose some of that anxiety. At least I hope so. Now let's all try to remember this the next time it storms".

One afternoon the children played out on the lawn and watched their mother and dad wash windows. Harry brought the ladder from the barn and he washed the outside as Alice did the inside. "I never saw a house with so many windows" said Alice.

Harry laughed. "The better to see you with, my dear" he said.

"Do you realize there are twelve of these big windows just on one side of this house?"

"Someone liked a lot of light I guess". Said Harry

She cleaned and polished until everything shined.

One morning just before Thanksgiving Mrs. Clary stopped Harry on the street "Hello" she said. "You are just the young man I wanted to see" she said.

"I need someone to help me butcher a few chickens. My flock has outgrown my hen house. I have decided to just put them in jars. That way I won't have to feed them, I hate to kill them" she said. "If you will come down and chop off the heads, you may take a couple of them home with you. They would make a good dinner."

Of course Harry helped her to butcher the chickens. She gave him three of the hens to take home. He had thought that she was killing off the hens that had quit laying eggs. But when he learned that she was giving him laying hens, Harry thought "Oh no, these chickens will not be dinner. They will be breakfast first." He was excited when he took home his prize.

He said "Irene, How would you like to help Daddy build a chicken coop?" Irene excitedly put on her shoes and coat and ran to help. She was really excited to be helping her dad make a chicken coop, When they had finished she thought it was a beautiful little chicken coop.

To Alice Harry said, "Honey, we could have chicken for Thanksgiving dinner, but these hens are still laying. I think it is better to keep them for the eggs. When spring comes, maybe we can find a rooster or buy a few eggs from Mrs. Clary and set them. We can set the hens and maybe enlarge our flock. We can sell the eggs if we have more than we can use."

Alice said, "I agree with you dear, "We don't need chicken for Thanksgiving. We will be thankful to have chickens to lay eggs."

Thanksgiving morning they woke to find a beautiful blanket of snow covering the ground. It was snowing beautiful big snowflakes. The children stood at the windows and watched it snow.

"Oh! It is so pretty" said Jean. "Daddy, can we go out and play?"

"Maybe after dinner we can go out for a little while".

"It is pretty cold out there. You will need to put on a lot of clothes, but maybe if you bundle up really well".

The little family had a Thanksgiving dinner of dried beans and fat back, with Alice's home made rolls and apple butter and enjoyed every bite.

After dinner Harry helped the children to put on their heaviest clothing, Harry found a couple of large boxes. He put little Harry and Jean in one box. He handed the other box to Irene and said, "Carry this to the top of that little hill over there". Harry walked up the hill carrying the box of children. It was cold, but the wind was calm. Even though it was cold, they had a lot of fun just sloshing through the snow. When they reached the top of the hill, Irene and Audrey crawled into one box and Harry pushed them to get the box started down the hill. As it went flying down the hill the girls squealed with delight. The other box was following right behind, with the other two children laughing and giggling.

When they reached the bottom, they were all yelling. "Let's do it again. Let's do it again"?

"Come on", said their dad, maybe a couple more times". So they all climbed to the top again. Harry allowed them to slide down the hill several times. Little Harry's nose was starting to get red from the cold. Harry knew it was time to go back indoors. The children really did not have clothing warm enough for this kind of fun.

"Okay!" Harry said. "This is the last time. We need to go to the house, and then inside". With a lot of squeals, and laughing, they took one last ride down the hill.

"After we get warmed up, maybe we can coax Mama into coming with us. We will hook up Old Bessie, and take a buggy ride. I'll bet even Mama would like that".

"Oh! Mama", Audrey said when they were safely indoors. "It was so much fun. We went sled riding".

"Come in and get those wet clothes off" said Alice. "I hope you won't catch a cold from all this fun".

"Oh! Mama we had so much fun" said Irene "Daddy said we can go for a buggy ride after we get warmed up. Do you want to go with us"?

"I don't think so. Little Harry is ready to go to sleep".

"We can bundle him in blankets" said Harry. "He will enjoy it too. You need to get out in this. It will do you good too. Come on Honey, live a little".

Alice finally gave in, and while she was dressing the children again in as many clothes as their little bodies could carry, Harry went out to get the buggy. They all climbed into the buggy, and off they rode. Soon the children were all fast asleep and even Alice was nodding off. "I really did enjoy this" she said. "But I am dead tired. It is such a beautiful night but let's call it a day"

"Ok!" joked Harry, "but are we going to call it a day or a night"?

"You were always a smart aleck" said Alice.

Harry carried the children inside one at a time and Alice undressed them and put them to bed.

Chapter 6

In the days that followed, Alice managed to find the time to make a dress for Mrs. Marley. What little she earned from her sewing went into the cup of change she was saving for Christmas.

Christmas was approaching fast, but there was no extra money for Santa. Alice spent all the time she could making dolls and doll clothes. Harry found some old lumber that had been piled behind the barn. He built a crib for the new baby who would soon be here. Alice wondered why Harry spent so much time in the barn. He told her that he was building surprises. He built some small furniture. There were four chairs and a small table. He also built a child size cupboard. He cleaned the empty room in the barn, and put the furniture in. It looked like a room for midgets. He pulled the door shut, and locked it. He didn't want this room to be found until Christmas.

Alice was finishing up the costumes which the girls would be wearing in the Christmas pageant at the church. The girls were all to be angels in the angel choir. There were fourteen little girls in the angel choir. Audrey was to be the soloist this year. She was so proud. She practiced almost all the time. There were several songs to be sung by the choir, and then Audrey would sing 'Away in a Manger'. Alice knew that she would be the proudest mother in the church that night if she were able to be there. It was nearly time for this baby to arrive, and Alice thought it would be just her luck to be stuck at home while everyone else in town would be listening to her daughter sing the solo in the Christmas pageant. She hoped she was wrong. But she had a feeling that she would not be in the audience that night.

Ten days before Christmas there was quite a commotion at the Jackson place. It had been arranged that when Alice's time came, Harry would take the children to Mabel's as soon as the first labor pains came. It was snowing hard, and since Harry didn't have a car, he would have to use the old horse and buggy. That would leave Alice alone for at least an hour. But it couldn't be helped. At about eight thirty in the evening Alice told Harry. "It's time. Get the kids and go. Tell Mabel I will need Ed before morning." Alice was not worried. She had had four children already, so she knew there was plenty of time. Ed would need to travel from Linwood, so he needed to be called right away. It would take him at least an hour to get here. Alice knew there was plenty of time, but she didn't want to waste any of it.

Harry said "Come on kids, you are going to spend the night with Aunt Mabel" Alice helped them get into pajamas, and put their coats on. They always liked to go to Aunt Mabel's, but they were sleepy and tired. They didn't understand why they were to be taken out in the cold so late at night. "Why do we have to go tonight?" "Can't we go in the morning" Alice lost patience with them because Jean was crying, and Irene had a tantrum. Harry said "Here Irene, carry this blanket you will need it. It's cold out there. Audrey you take this blanket. Don't drag it.

Carrying little Harry and Jean he went out the door with the children. As he helped them into the buggy, he told them "Maybe tomorrow we will have a surprise for you."

"Is Santa coming tonight?" Jean asked. "No" said Harry "It isn't quite time for Santa but you will see tomorrow." By the time they got settled and bundled up in the blankets, they were satisfied and enjoyed the ride.

The children were all asleep when Harry arrived at Mabel's so, picking up little Harry he ran in to tell Mabel to call Ed. Mabel's daughter, Margaret, happened to be home visiting at the time.

44

Margaret went with Harry to go back out to the buggy and carry in a child. By the time they got there, Irene was awake and getting out of the buggy. Margaret carried Jean and Harry took Audrey into the house. Jean woke up and started to cry, "I want my Mommy." She said, "Where is Mommy?"

It's ok sweetheart" said Harry, "You were asleep in the buggy. You are at Aunt Mabel's. You are going to sleep here tonight".

Mabel immediately called her husband and told him it was time for Alice. He replied that he would be on the way in five minutes. Mabel asked Margaret to put the children to bed. She said "I will go out with Harry. Alice shouldn't be alone for too long at a time like this. If your father stops here" she told Margaret "tell him we have gone. Tell him to hurry." And with that she and Harry left the house in a hurry.

In the meantime, Alice was walking the floor. She had walked for what seemed like hours. Suddenly she began to realize that something was different. Something must have gone wrong. The pains were coming harder, and faster than she remembered with the other children. She expected to have a couple of hours before they became this strong. All of a sudden she was frightened. "Maybe I should lie down" she thought. "Maybe that will slow things down a little. I can't have this baby alone". It seemed to her that Harry had been gone for hours. She cried a little, and then she laughed at herself because she knew that was no help. She lay down, but she couldn't lie still. She screamed "Oh! God Help me. I can't have this baby alone. Please God send someone to help me". What could she do, she was all alone.

Finally she told herself "You have done this before. You have to calm down. Remember what Mabel always says. Stop and think. You need to stop and think when something goes wrong. What would Mabel do? Just stop being so childish and have this baby. Finally she realized there was only one thing she could do.

She lay down on the bed and started to push. She gave a couple of huge pushes, and Mabel heard a baby's cry as she came in the door. Rushing to Alice's side Mabel took the baby and tended to it. "It's another girl" she said. She immediately went about taking care of Alice and the baby. Being a doctor's wife, she had done this many times. She bathed the baby, and swaddled her. Then cleaned and straightened the room. She laid her next to her mother in the bed. Both mother and baby were soon asleep.

The weather was getting bad when Ed left Linwood. His car kept sliding this way and that, so he was finally forced to stop to put on chains. He had a lot of trouble getting them on; he had never had to do this before. It seemed that he worked for hours to no avail. Finally a man stopped. "Doctor," he said, "What are you doing out on a night like this?" He was one of the miners who worked in Linwood. Ed did not know who he was, but was certainly glad he was there. "My sister-in-law is having a baby and I was rushing to deliver it. I hope my wife has gone to her because she may not wait for me. These little ones have a mind of their own."

"We'll have you on the road in no time flat" said the stranger. Within a few minutes the man and his son had the chains on Ed's car.

"There you go" said the man. "You be careful Doctor, It is a bad night to be on the road"

:"Thank You" said Ed. "How much do I owe you?"

"Nothing" said the stranger, "If my wife needed you I would hope someone would do the same for me." Ed reached into his pocket and handed the man a dollar. "Times are rough" he said. "Thank you very much."

With that Ed got into his car and drove off. It was snowing very hard and it was all he could do to see where he was driving. It was a narrow unpaved road, and very slippery. Ed drove at a snail's pace but finally reached Elkton. He thought "I can't take the time to stop for Mabel. I hope I am not too late. I hope Mabel has gone out there already. I must get right out to Harry's. Alice is a very flighty, nervous and panicky woman. If she is alone she will be in a real state. At least I hope Harry is with her, He does have a calming affect on her."

When Ed reached the house, the baby had been bathed and

swaddled, and the mother and baby were both sleeping. The doctor examined the baby, assured everyone that she was a healthy little girl, and sat down to drink a cup of coffee.

By the time Mabel and Harry were ready to leave for home, the snow had drifted around the car so badly that there would be no moving it until someone shoveled it out of there. They were all too tired for that tonight. "Let's get some rest first" Harry said. "You can sleep in the kid's bed tonight and I will get you back on the road first thing in the morning." Since everyone was dog tired they all went to bed and slept soundly until morning.

As soon as daylight came, Harry went to the barn and brought in the new crib. Alice was surprised and happy. "I won't have to take little Harry out of the crib. He can stay in it for awhile. That will make my life a little easier. But Harry, how did you manage to get the wood to build this? I know you didn't have any money."

"There was a pile of lumber behind the barn" answered Harry. "I asked Joe what it was for, and he said it was left over from some remodeling they did a year or so ago. He said if I could find a use for it, to go ahead. So I found a use for it."

"Oh Harry" said Alice "It is beautiful. Mabel, can you help me to make a pad for it. There is a blanket in the upstairs closet. We could sew a couple of layers together. If you go up and get the blanket, and get me a needle and thread from my sewing basket in the laundry room, I will start on it right away."

Harry said "While you ladies are doing that, I will get a shovel and get Ed's car out of that snow drift. Then I will hook up old Bessie, and we will break the road open so that you people can get back home.

He went out to shovel the doctor's car out of the snow drift. It had stopped snowing and the sun was shining. Harry then hooked Bessie up to a plow, and led the way, clearing the road. Although it was very cold it was a beautiful wintry day. Mabel and Ed then followed Harry back to town.

"The children will stay with me for the next few days. Don't worry about them. They will need some clothes though so be sure to bring them some tomorrow."

"I will" Said Harry", Thank you both for everything".

Chapter 7

As Harry drove the wagon back to the house he thought over the events of last night. Poor Alice was alone when the baby came. She must have been frantic. Even though she had other babies before, it must have been scary for her to be all alone at that time. He was really glad that he and Mabel got home when they did. Knowing Alice as he did, he couldn't help but wonder what she would have done if they had not come when they did. Alice had a way of always doing the wrong thing in a crisis. "I really do love you Alice, but you really worry me sometimes" he thought to himself.

Harry went back to be with Alice. "I'm sorry you were all alone when the baby came he said. "I know you must have been frightened."

"I was at first. I nearly went out of my mind... But do you know what I thought about. I thought of Mabel giving me the devil. And how she keeps telling me to stop and think. Then I realized I had to do it, and I was doing the best I knew how. But I sure was glad to see Mabel when she came in that door. And Honey I made some stuff too" Alice said. "I made a dress for Mrs. Richards. She paid me two dollars. I am making one for Mrs. Friend too. If she will give me a dollar or two, I think we can get the kids a pair of shoes for Christmas. I made them each a dress. I cut down a couple of my dresses, and made each of the girls one. I made some doll clothes from some scraps I had. And I also made each of them a new rag doll. I hope I can talk Audrey into giving up that raggedy thing she plays with. It is so dirty and raggedy it is not fit for a child. But I don't know that even a new dolly will encourage her to give this one up. I have three dollars that I stashed away last month, and with what I have earned we should have about eight dollars to spend for Christmas. I think if we buy each of them a pair of shoes, and get some fruit and nuts for the stockings. Mr. Walters will give you a few cents worth of candy when you pay the grocery bill this week. I think we can have a right nice Christmas. Thank God we live out here in the country and the kids won't see what other children get. By the time Irene goes back to school there will not be too much talk about it. I am glad they won't know what they are missing.

"They are young" said Harry. "But honey, I hate to see you using your clothes to make clothes for the kids. Soon you won't have anything nice to wear. I also don't think most of the other children in town will be getting very much either. Everyone is hurting this year. I think Irene is the only one of ours who is old enough to remember anyway. Honey, I promise you that the first job that comes along will be mine. I am looking and listening all the time. If I can find anything at all, I can still do what needs to be done around here. We will be on easy street if I can just find something with a nice paycheck at the end of the week. I am so sorry that I have disappointed you lately."

"Oh! Harry" Alice said. "It is not your fault. I am not disappointed with you. I know you do your best. You can't make a silk purse out of a sow's ear. You know that. Times are hard and we will just have to hope they get better soon. I know you will get a job soon."

Alice and Harry spent the rest of the week alone in the house. Of course Alice was in bed. Ed had said she needed to spend the next ten days in bed. That was why Mabel was keeping the children. When the weekend came Mabel brought them out to see their new sister. "What is her name Mama?" asked Irene. "Can I hold her?"

"We named her Mary" said Alice. "We will have a merry Christmas, Right?"

"Oh Mama" said Irene, "Will we spell her name M-e-r-r-y?"

"No dear, I forgot you are big enough to know the difference. We will spell her name M-a-r-y, but she will help us to have an M-e-r-r-y Christmas. Okay?"

"Okay Mama"

The children were all talking at once. Each took a turn holding their new sister.

"Now Daddy" said Jean. "When do we get our puppy? You said we could have a new baby and a puppy when we moved, remember." Alice laughed.

"So I did" said Harry with a wink to Alice. "I'm working on that. We will see if maybe Santa has one." Alice turned to Harry. "We can't afford a puppy" she whispered.

"But it would have to be a small puppy that would not grow up to be too big. Mama says it would eat too much" said Harry. "Remember I am not promising that we will get a puppy right soon. I am just saying I am working on it. Sometimes we have to wait for nice things and this may be one thing we will have to wait for."

"I hope we don't have to wait too long" said Jean. "I would love to have a puppy."

"Well girls" said Mabel. "It is time for us to go back to town. Your mama needs her rest. Uncle Ed said she is to get a lot of rest so that she can care for all of you and a new baby too."

Do I have to go?" Irene begged. "I can help Mama with the baby. Can't I stay here with Mama? I am a big girl now."

"No sweetheart" said her mother. "I know you are a big girl. That is why I really need you to go with Aunt Mabel to help her with the little ones. You will do that for me won't you?"

"How long do we have to stay there?" Irene asked.

"I promise it will just be for a few more days." said her mother. "You need to go to school for a couple more days anyway. At Aunt Mabel's you only need to walk across the street to the school. It is cold and snowy out there and it will be nicer for you too. When school closes for Christmas, you will all come back home. How does that sound?"

"Okay Mama"

"Oh by the way" said Mabel "Next Sunday is the pageant at the church" said Mabel. "Were you able to get the angel costumes finished?"

"Yes said Alice they are hanging on the door in the laundry room. You can take them with you if you want to" I won't be able to attend, but their dad will be there. He wouldn't miss it for the world.

"You bettcha" said their dad. "I wouldn't miss it for the world.

The three older girls were to be angels in the Christmas pageant. They were so proud. With that the children then quietly left with Mabel. Harry and Alice were again alone. Alice immediately turned on Harry. "Why did you promise them a puppy? You know we barely have enough food for them. We can't afford a dog too. A dog eats as much as a child."

"Earl's dog had a litter just before Thanksgiving. She has three of the cutest little rat terrier pups you ever saw. He said. I could have one, and they are just about ready to leave their mother. I think we have enough table scraps for a small dog like that. And I was hoping that it would fill the void at Christmas time."

"Oh! I know it would make them so happy. I don't like to sound so mean, but I don't think we can afford it, even if it is free.

"What if I stop and get Mabel's scraps too? I know I can feed a puppy without taking food from my children. I promise that if it becomes a problem I will give the dog away."

"After the kids have become attached to it? Oh! Harry you know we couldn't do that."

"Think about it for a few days. I won't bring it home if you tell me not to. But think about it dear. I want a puppy too. I will be as disappointed as the kids if we can't have a puppy."

Alice knew she was out numbered. She told him that she would have to think about it but she knew that by Christmas day, there would be another mouth to feed.

Mabel brought the children home just three days before Christmas. They were all excited with news about what they had done at Aunt Mabel's. They had enjoyed their time there. They had helped her to trim her tree. It was a great big tree. Mabel had a large living room with fourteen foot ceilings. She usually had a tree that was ten or twelve feet high. She had a lot of fancy ornaments she had saved over the years. She usually had one of the most beautiful trees in town. She decorated inside and out. Her porch looked like a winter wonderland. She loved decorating, and went overboard, especially when the children were there to help her.

Mabel loved those children, but spoiled them a lot. Alice was thankful every day for Mabel. Without her, Alice knew that her own life would be harder than it now was. Mabel was a wonderful friend as well as Harry's sister. And having a doctor in the family was also a blessing. She wondered sometimes what they would do without Mabel and Ed.

The girls went out to help Harry gather the eggs and feed the chickens. That gave Alice time to talk to Mabel. She told Mabel that Harry wanted to get one of Earl's puppies for Christmas. She also told her that she was worried about another mouth to feed. "I would love to get the kids a dog but a dog eats as much as a child. I try so hard to keep food on the table. I know Harry does his best, but our family is getting bigger and our income keeps getting smaller. I don't know what to do."

"Alice" said Mabel. "One of those small dogs like Earl has eats about a handful of food a day. Harry is right the kids probably drop that much food on the floor every day. And think about the look on your kid's faces on Christmas morning if there is a new little puppy to love. I think you should get it. I know you worry, but let this one go. I don't think you will be sorry."

"I knew I would have to do this" said Alice. "But you are right. I worry too much sometimes."

When Harry and the children came in from outside Audrey said,

"Mama, we only have three chickens, but we got four eggs today"

"Boy, one of our hens is doing double duty I guess. Maybe she just wanted to give you a Christmas present". They all laughed.

Mabel said "I brought a couple dozen cookies. Why don't we have some milk and cookies and we can tell your Mama about all the things we did at my house" Then turning to Alice she said "I think I would rather have a nice cup of hot tea, if you have some, if not, coffee will be ok.

The children were all talking at once telling Alice about what they had done at Aunt Mabel's. They had made cookies, and decorated the tree. Aunt Mabel had a big Santa on the door. He was almost as big as Daddy. Aunt Mabel had a lot of packages under her tree. Alice loved the sparkle in the kid's eyes as they talked about Christmas. She wondered if they could be any happier if Santa was really going to bring them all kinds of pretty things.

Mabel had given them a few decorations that she had left over and they wanted to decorate everything. "Wait until we get our own tree to decorate" said Harry.

"Are we going to have a tree too?" asked Audrey.

"Of course we will have a tree. It won't be as elaborate as Aunt Mabel's, but it will be our very own little tree. We can make decorations and trim it ourselves".

Now I think it is time for all of you to go to bed. We have a busy time the next few days.

After the children were in bed Mabel said "Joe called me today. He wanted me to tell you that he will be home sometime tomorrow. He said that Marge knows that you have probably not been able to do anything to the house, but she says that will be fine. If you want I can run in and dust a little. I know that you had really given it a good cleaning, so it can't be bad.

"I don't think it is too bad but if you can dust the bedroom I can do the downstairs. There is really not anything pressing. Everything almost shines"

"Ok You shouldn't be taking the stairs yet, so I will do that. It will only take a jiffy"

Harry said. "This will be the first time we ever met Marge. Joe says she really doesn't like to come home because it makes her so nostalgic. She misses her mother when she comes here. He said he thinks they should sell the place, but Marge throws a fit every time he mentions it".

"I know how she feels" said Alice "My mother has been gone for almost ten years, and I still miss her every time I go to the farm. It will never be the same again. But it seems like I can feel her there sometimes."

Mabel and Alice spent about ten minutes in the front of the house and it really did shine. Alice said "I know Marge would understand if it were a little dusty. But I am glad that I did have time to clean it nice before I had the baby. I'm glad I didn't wait until I knew when they were coming"

"Well she will have nothing to complain about I am sure of that. Joe didn't say if they were bringing anyone with them, did he?"

"No he didn't say. I think it will be just he and Marge. But I did dust the round room and that one small bedroom too just in case. But even if they do bring guests, there isn't enough dust to worry about. And Marge should know that you are not supposed to take the stairs yet"

"Okay let's call it a day then". Mabel left for home and Alice picked up her knitting. She had made three pairs of mittens while she was in bed after the baby came. She was on the last pair.

Chapter 8

Joe and Marge came in around noon the next day. Harry had cleaned the porch furniture and brought it from the barn. Joe said "You really didn't have to do that. It is usually too cold to sit on the porch during Christmas".

"I know, but I just thought maybe we will have at least one nice day while you are here. If not, we can take it back to the barn for a few more months".

Harry and Joe sat on the porch for awhile that day. Harry told Joe how Bessie had surely come in handy several times. "Even if I had a car, I would not have been able to get in and out of here sometimes. We have fallen in love with that old horse. We don't ride her much, but the kids love to ride in the buggy"

"I'm glad you like her" said Joe.

"We will be going to church in the buggy tonight" Harry said. "The kids are in the Christmas pageant. They are really excited about it"

"I thought we should put up a Christmas tree, but since we are only staying for three days, Marge thinks it is a waste of time. I was glad, because I hate that mess especially when we don't have enough time to enjoy it".

"I know what you mean. I think if it were not for the kids we wouldn't even have one. But I want them to have as nice a Christmas as I can provide".

"Yes, Christmas is for kids" said Joe.

"Marge and I would not have even come home this year, but her brother has asked us to Christmas dinner, and we don't see the family much any more so we decided to come.

The Christmas pageant at the church was a huge success. Harry was at the church early so that Mabel could help the girls into their costumes. The church was crowded. It seemed that everybody in town was there that evening. Even people who didn't usually come to church were there to see their little ones perform. Parents and Grandparents were all there to see what these children had been up to for the last six or eight weeks. The new minister had been gathering with them almost every evening. This was to be the greatest production of the year. People had never seen these kids so excited about anything for awhile. Children who were usually fighting among themselves were working together to make this show a success. It seemed that this minister had a magic touch with the kids in Elkton. There seemed to be a change in attitude. The bullies were suddenly becoming pussy cats.

Alice's daughters were part of the angel choir. They sang several Christmas songs. There were fourteen little girls in the children's choir. They had practiced for weeks. They were so proud. Audrey sang a solo 'Away in A Manger'. Harry sat in the audience and almost cried as his little girl sang her song. He could not have been more proud. He wished his wife could be here to hear this. Of course she had heard Audrey sing many times, but this time she was dressed like an angel, and she looked like an angel up there on that stage with all of those other little angels. Harry's heart nearly burst with pride.

All of the children of the church were in the play. Everyone had a part. There were little skits, poetry recitals, story readers, and lots of songs. The minister read from the bible, the story of the Christ Child's birth. And it was dramatized by the children. Although it was a serious reenactment, there were a lot of laughs and chuckles from the adults who were watching entranced with these actors. Each and every parent in the church that evening watched spellbound as their child or children did his or her part to entertain them. Everybody laughed when the child who was the 'Christ Child' crawled out of the manger and ran down the aisle in the church crying for his mama. Joey Barkley tried to hold him down to keep him in the manger, but he slapped Joey and ran anyway.

At the end of the evening Santa showed up with a bag of candy for each of the little ones. Each child sat on Santa's lap and told Santa what he or she wanted for Christmas. Most of them asked for new shoes, and boots. Most of these children had already learned that toys are not the most important things in a child's life.

When the pageant was over Harry gathered his little tribe together, and piled them all in the buggy. By the time they reached home they were all asleep. Harry woke Irene and Audrey. They gathered up their blankets and trudged to the house. By the time they were inside they were wide awake. He carried Jean inside and put her on the couch. The girls told Alice about their evening. "Mama" said Irene. "You should have seen little James Browning; He was supposed to be the Christ Child, in the manger. When the pastor was about half way through the story, James crawled out of the Manger and ran down the aisle of the church crying for his Mama. It was so funny. Everybody laughed, even Reverend Baker. We should have had little Mary there. She couldn't get out of the manger".

"I'll bet that was a sight to see. I wish I could have been there. I am sure it was a great show.

"Yes it was" said Audrey. "Maybe you can go next year Mama",

Maybe I can" said Alice. "Now it is time to go to bed if you are going to help your dad get a Christmas tree tomorrow.

The next morning Alice gave Harry what money she had

She told him to buy each of the kids a pair of shoes. "I wish we could afford boots but that is out of the question this time. Maybe we can find a pair of used boots for Irene before the weather gets too much worse. They love to play in the snow and we have two girls in school next year I surely hope we can get them both boots before that.". She told him what size shoes each of them should wear. Harry went to town to do the Christmas shopping.

When he returned he took the three older girls out in the woods and cut down a small pine tree. He made a big production of finding just the right tree. The girls wanted to get the biggest tree they could find, but Harry explained that it would take too much to trim it. "If we get a big tree it will look sickly with just a little trimming, but a little tree will look all fat and sassy when we make decorations and put them on it. Mama will be pleased."

"We need just a little tree, so that we can decorate it pretty for Mama" he told them. They spend about half an hour looking for just the right tree. This one was too skinny, that one was too short and squatty, that one was too big. Finally, they found just the right tree for Mama.

They took the tree into the house shaking it well on the porch to get most of the snow off. Harry set the tree up in a corner of the parlor. Alice found a magazine with a lot of color on the pages. She helped the children to cut strips of paper, and showed them how to paste the strips together with flour and water paste, to make chains. The girls worked for several hours making chains and eating popcorn which Harry popped. Alice strung some of the popcorn on long chains. Of course they ate more than Alice could string. But they had a good time.

They all sang Christmas carols around the tree. The fire in the fireplace crackled. Alice thought it was a beautiful sight seeing her family so happy. She couldn't help feeling a little sad though. She was glad that they didn't know how much they were really missing.

Alice had made some cookies that morning. She allowed each child to decorate two cookies for the tree. Each girl spread her cookies with red frosting. Then Irene wrote their names on their cookies with white frosting. Even Little Harry, who would soon be two years old, decorated one cookie. He had more red frosting on himself than the cookie. The girls laughed, but they had plenty of frosting to lick off their fingers too.

They made snowflakes from newspaper. Irene had learned to make them in school and she taught the others how to do it. They even pasted some snowflakes on the windows. They decorated everything. Harry went out and brought in a few pine cones which he had dipped into white paint. They had just the slightest bit of white, making them look like it had snowed on them.

When the tree was 'beautifully' trimmed Alice gave each child a sock which was hung very carefully on the mantel.

"Does Santa really come down the chimney Daddy?" asked Jean. "If he does, we need to let the fire go out."

"Santa will know if there is a fire in the fireplace. And he will come down the other chimney."

"How will he know where our stockings are?"

"Santa will know. He knows everything" said their mother. "Now I think you had better get to bed or Santa will not come at all."

After the children were tucked into bed, Harry went out to the barn and brought in the cutest little puppy. It was not much bigger than a kitten. It was a brown sandy color with a small white spot on his tail. He put the puppy on Alice's lap. Alice immediately fell in love. The puppy licked her face, and she laughed.

"Oh! She said. You are the cutest little thing I ever saw. I don't know if we can afford you, little fellow" she said. "But welcome to our family."

I am going to put him in a box behind the kitchen stove for the night. I hope he doesn't cry and wake up the kids"

"Here" said Alice. She filled a pint jar with warm water from the reservoir in the stove. She wrapped it in a towel. Then she handed Harry a clock.

"Put these in the box too" she said. "The warm bottle is warm like his mother. The clock's ticking is like his mother's heartbeat. He will be snug as a bug in a rug."

"How do you know all this stuff?" asked Harry with a chuckle.

"I was raised on a farm, remember. But the kids are upstairs and

I doubt that they will hear him even if he does cry. But I am sure I would."

Alice put the things she had made for the children under the tree with the four pairs of shoes. She wished she had more, but that was all she could afford. She was glad they were so young. Maybe they would not remember getting so little for Christmas. That night she prayed that next year would be better.

Chapter 9

Harry was glad he had not told Alice about his surprise in the barn. She would be pleased he knew, and it would be a great surprise for her as well as the children. He couldn't wait to see the look on her face when she saw what he had done. He was really pleased when he fell into bed that night. He knew that even though it wasn't much, he had done the best he could for his family.

He prayed that next year would be better.

Harry awoke before dawn on Christmas morning. He quietly got out of bed and dressed. He wanted to have the house warm when Alice and the children woke to come downstairs. He built a fire in the kitchen stove and put on the coffee pot. He also built a fire in the fireplace. He took the box with the puppy into the parlor and hid it behind a chair. When Alice woke, she smelled the coffee. She got up and went downstairs.

After pouring herself a cup of coffee and tasting it, she said "This coffee tastes really good this morning".

"It was made by the master chef" Harry shrewdly remarked.

"Maybe the master chef should work here more often" Alice said with a smile.

They heard the children starting to stir. Audrey was awake first. Alice heard her say "Irene, Jean, come on. Get up. Let's go down and see if Santa came." There was a lot of bustling on the stairs. The girls came running downstairs. Alice went up to get little Harry from the crib. She told the children that they must get dressed and eat breakfast before they could go into the parlor and find out what Santa brought. They insisted they were not hungry, but their mother was very strict about breakfast.

Alice cooked oatmeal and made toast for breakfast. The children gobbled it up. They were anxious to see what was beyond that door. They were so excited. Alice again got a guilty feeling. She thought, "They are so excited, and there is really nothing for them." She wanted to cry but she knew that would only make things worse. When they had finished eating Harry opened the parlor door. Under the tree were four beautiful rag dolls, and a rubber ball. Each child had a new pair of shoes. Each girl had a new dress and little Harry had a new shirt made with love from one of his dad's old ones. The children were all as excited as if they had real treasure. Alice then allowed herself to shed a few tears. "They are so young" she thought. "I am so glad they don't know what they are missing."

"Oh! Mama" said Irene. "It's yellow. You knew I wanted a yellow dress didn't you?"

Hugging the new dress in her arms, the little girl ran to her mother and hugged her. Alice cried again. Then Harry pulled the box from behind the chair. The children all jumped up and down giggling and laughing.

"Our puppy" they all cried at once. "Santa brought us a puppy. Oh! Daddy, he is so cute. Let me hold him." Then they all wanted to hold the puppy at once. Harry allowed each of them to hold the puppy for a little while. Then he explained that the puppy was just a baby, and they could not handle him too much. "It could make the puppy sick if we handle him too much at first. He has to get used to living with us".

"Just like Little Mary" he said. "He needs a lot of rest so he can grow."

"Right now I think he needs something to eat" said Alice.

She took the puppy to the kitchen and put some of the oatmeal in a bowl. She put in a little milk and set the bowl on the floor. The puppy lapped it up.

"We must think of a name for him. We will take the day today to think about it... Each of us will come up with one name. This evening Daddy will help decide which name is best." She said and smiled at Harry. She wondered how he would decide on a name for this dog.

The children all started calling off names they liked. "Rover" "Blackie" "Bowser" "Joie" "doggie."

"You must think about this all day" said Alice. "Each of you may think of one name. He can go for one day without a name. Think about it today and tonight we will name our puppy."

As they quieted down a little Harry said "Now everybody needs to put on their coat and hat, even you, Mommy. We are going for a walk. I have something I want to show all of you."

Alice said "I can't leave the baby. You can take the children."

"No" said Harry. "Five minutes is all this will take. The baby is asleep, and I will only need five minutes of your time. Come on dear, I need you to do this for us."

Alice reluctantly put on her coat and said "Well let's hurry. I must hurry back inside."

Harry carried Little Harry, and led the whole family to the barn. He unlocked the door to his special room. Three little girls squealed with delight as Alice took in a deep breath. "Oh! Harry" she said. "How and when did you do all this?"

"I know that until the weather gets nicer it won't get much use. But I think every little girl needs a playhouse. My little girls will be no exception. When spring comes they will have the best darned playhouse in Elkton."

"They certainly will" said Alice. "It is beautiful. Now girls you may stay out here with your dad for a little while. I must get back to Mary" and she hurried back to the house.

"Daddy" said Irene "I think this is the nicest Christmas ever. Look kids, we even have a cupboard. Maybe next Christmas Santa will bring us some dishes.

Each of the girls sat down on a chair and pretended to be drinking. "Daddy, can we stay here and play house for a little while please?"

"You may stay for a little while. It is pretty cold out here, so your Mama will want you inside soon" Harry said. "See that bell there on the side of the barn." They all turned to look for the bell. There, on the side of the barn was a big cow bell.

"There is a wire fastened to that bell". He said "When your mother wants you to come indoors she will ring that bell. You must come inside when the bell rings".

"Oh! Daddy" said Irene. "You are the best daddy in the whole wide world."

Harry returned to the house and explained to Alice about the bell. He showed her a hook on the back porch with a wire attached. The wire led to the barn where the bell was attached. "Pull on the wire, and the bell will ring. The children should come running."

"Well, what will you think of next?" Alice asked. "And I thought you had lost your mind telling the children they could play that far from the house."

"Alice" said Harry "We have to let them grow up. Irene is almost ten and Audrey will be six in March. If you ring the bell, and they don't come immediately we will punish them. They will learn responsibility. I think they will be fine out there for a few hours at a time once the weather gets warm enough. If you start to worry about them, you can call them in just by ringing the bell."

"You are usually right dear" Alice said. "I do worry too much sometimes. I know I do. But now I think it is a little too cold out there. Why don't you ring that bell and see if it works". Harry pulled on the wire, ringing the bell, and the girls came running in from the barn.

"Oh! Mama" said Irene. "We are going to have so much fun when summer comes. I can't Wait until Mary Helen comes. She loves to play house",

That evening, after the children were in their pajamas, ready for bed, Harry said "isn't there something we are all forgetting?"

For a moment all was silent. Then Harry picked up the puppy. "Oh! Yes" they all said in unison. "We need to name our puppy." Each child yelled out several names, all yelling at once.

"Whoa! Ho!" said their dad. "Remember we each get to choose one name. Mama, get a pencil and paper. We will have a regular election". Mama found a pencil and a piece of paper.

"Now Harry, what do you think we should name our puppy?"

"I want to call him 'Fuzzy'" said little Harry. He's a fuzzy little puppy."

"That's a nice name" said his dad. "Now, Jean what is your suggestion?"

Jean said "I think he should be named 'Pal', because he is so friendly, and he follows me around. He can be my pal."

"Okay, that's great Audrey, what do you want to call him?"

"Can we call him 'Rover'? That is a nice name for a dog."

"Yes it is a nice name" "What about you Irene do you have a good name?"

"There is a dog in a story I read last week. His name is 'Laddie'. I like that name. Could we name him that"?

"Alright, we have 'Fuzzy', 'Pal', 'Rover' and 'Laddie'" Mama, do you want to make a suggestion?"

"I don't think so" said Mama. "I think all of those names are very nice."

"Okay Mama, write each name on a piece of paper and put them in my hat" said Harry handing his hat to Alice. "Shake them up, and I will draw out a name. That will be what we will call our new puppy."

Yeah! The children all yelled and danced with glee.

Alice wrote each name on a piece of paper. She folded each piece neatly and put them into their father's hat. Then she held the hat out to Harry, and with much fanfare, he chose one, and having done so he ceremoniously handed it to Alice. She took her time unfolding the paper. All eyes were on that little piece of paper. Finally, after a great amount of time Alice announced "Our new puppies name is "Fuzzy.""

All the children wanted to hold the puppy and call him by his chosen name. After a lot of oh's and ahs Alice announced. "And now I think it is time for bed. Let me hear the patter of tiny feet going up those stairs. I will be up in a jiffy to tuck all of you in."

After the children were all in bed, Alice went up to kiss them each goodnight.

"Mama" said Jean. Will you read us a story"?

"Okay" said Alice, "but just a short one. I have a few things I must do before I go to bed. We have played so much today that I still have to finish some work".

"Mama we have had so much fun today. Thank you for the nice Christmas. I love you" said Irene.

"I love you too" the other children said in unison.

By the time Alice had finished the story every one of the children had fallen asleep. She kissed them all again and tip-toed back down the stairs.

Chapter 10

It was a very hard winter, very cold and it seemed that it snowed almost every day. Irene spent a lot of nights at Aunt Mabel's. When she was able to walk home in the evening, Harry tried to walk with her whenever he could.

Sometimes Harry would dress the kids all up and wrap them in blankets. He would hook Old Bessie to the wagon, and off they would go. They might go to visit Aunt Mabel, or sometimes he took them with him when he went to the store for a few groceries. Sometimes they would just ride around the barn and house a few times. All the while they would be singing. They all loved to sing, and Alice had taught them a lot of songs. Alice had a voice like an angel, but Harry's always said he could not carry a tune in a bucket with a lid on. And he was right, but he liked to sing anyway. And the children liked to sing with him.

They liked to play in the snow, but they got cold very quickly. When it was not snowing it was usually even colder than when it snowed. Without really good clothing, and good boots, playing in the cold was not very much fun. Most of the winter had to be spent near the cozy fireplace.

Alice was determined that at least Irene and Audrey would have warm clothing for next winter. Both girls would be in school next year, and somehow she would make sure that they at least had good warm boots on their feet. Each time she made an article of clothing for someone, she would put ten of fifteen cents in a pint jar she had tucked in the back of her kitchen cupboard. She could make them nice coats hats and mittens if she could find decent materials. But they also needed a good pair of boots. Wading through the snow without boots was not good for them. They would have to walk the two miles to school, and if their dad was able to find work before then, they would have to walk alone. This year Harry always walked with Irene to school on bad days. But hopefully he would be working before next winter. Oh! How she prayed for that.

Alice often thought that they should have never moved so far out of town. It would have been much better for Irene if she did not have to walk so far to school. But she also wondered what the other option could have been. She knew there was no other option. Sometimes when it was especially cold and snowy Harry would take her to school in the buggy. But he did not want her to get used to that because if and when he got a job, she would have to walk. He wanted her to know that she would not always have that option either. Irene did not mind walking to school, and she even liked to walk to school with her Dad, but if she had to walk alone, she sometimes had to walk through the cemetery, and it was scary. Daddy told her nothing would hurt her there, and she was sure he was right, but it seemed a little spooky in the evening when it was starting to get dark. Sometimes she would cry, but she would never tell her Daddy that. He thought she was a brave little girl. And she did not want him to learn how afraid she was.

The cute little play house in the barn did not get much use for months after Christmas. The girls would go out there occasionally and just sit for a few moments on their nice little chairs. But it was too cold to spend much time in the barn. Alice tried to allow the children to be outdoors for a little while each day, but they could not stay out for long. They would come back indoors crying because they were cold.

So far they had managed to keep the kids in shoes in the winter time, but boots were not in the budget. Winters were blustery in this part of the Maryland Mountains. There was no predicting when, or how much it would snow. Harry had been out of work for over a year now, with no prospect in sight. They were so lucky to have a roof over their head. If they had not taken this job, they would really have nothing. This job was supposed to supplement Harry's wages. It turned out to be his only wages. She had thought that Harry would find something long before this. It was almost Spring. They had four dollars a week plus a few cents here and there from her sewing and Harry's odd jobs. Alice thanked God that she had canned everything she could. Now she was thinking about spring. They must plant a bigger garden. Where would they find money for seeds? She had saved some seed from her own garden last year. But she would need a lot more.

One of the hardest tasks Alice did was the laundry. If possible, Harry usually stayed at home on laundry day to help her with the lifting of tubs of water. Sometimes she was forced to do it alone. One day early in the Spring he had stayed at home to help her. This was one job that he always tried to manage to help her with. They got up early in the morning, and she sorted her clothes. She washed baby clothes and diapers first. Since she had two babies in diapers she usually had quite a few of them to wash. One tub of cold water would get all the diapers ready for the wash board. Of course each time she changed a baby she would rinse the diaper and put it in a bucket with a lid. She usually washed baby clothes at least two or three times a week. They were the easiest. She didn't have enough diapers to last longer than a few days. After rubbing each piece of clothing on the wash board, Alice would put each piece of white clothing in the boiler. This was a large oval shaped vat which was set on the stove. The white clothes boiled in this vat for an hour or so. In the meantime, Alice would rub the colored clothes on the wash board. It was back breaking work. After each piece of clothing had been rubbed, soaked and rinsed. She would hang each piece to dry. By then the whites had boiled long enough. She would take them from the boiling water, and put them in a cold water rinse. Then wring them again and put them in another rinse tub. Each piece of white clothing was rinsed, wrung, rubbed, wrung, boiled, and then rinsed and wrung twice again. Then it was hung on the clothes line, hopefully out-of-doors. On rainy days Harry would string lines through the bedrooms during the day, and they were hung in-doors. Most of the time in winter they were dried in-doors. Each piece of colored and dark clothing was rubbed wrung, rinsed, wrung, rinsed and wrung again. Alice was always glad when spring came and she could dry all the clothes in the sunshine.

"This is a beautiful place in the spring" Alice told Harry as she hung the last of the clothes. Spring has such a fresh smell. Have you noticed how much fresher everything smells here today?"

"Yes" said Harry, "and listen to the birds. They are telling us that better times are coming. I hope they come soon. Alice, you are amazing. I know how hard this winter has been on you. Sometimes I hear you cry at night, and it breaks my heart. But you seldom complain. I would give anything if I could lighten your load some. There is not too much for me to do around here. I know that maybe there are things I could help you with but if I spend too much time around the house, I am so afraid I will miss out on that job I am so anxious to find. And at least if I can earn a quarter or so it helps some. When I get a job, I am going to buy you something really special, maybe a washing machine."

Alice giggled. "Don't spend all our money in the same place, but when that time comes, I won't complain if you buy me a washing machine. You can bet on that. But I think maybe there might be things we need worse" she said laughing.

A storm came up one Saturday afternoon. Irene, Audrey and Jean were in their playhouse. Irene said "it looks like it is going to storm, come on kids; we have to get to Mama."

"Maybe we could just stay here. Mama wouldn't come out here to get us would she?" said Audrey.

"Probably not, but she would go crazy, and that is not a good idea anyhow" said Irene. "Little Harry and Mary are in the house with Mama. Come on let's go before it starts to storm bad". On the way back to the house Irene said "Now what we want to do is what Daddy said. We need to stay calm and talk to Mama like she is the child and we are the adults. Do you girls think you can do that?"

"We will try, won't we Jean".

They reached the house just as it started to thunder. They heard Mama scream. She had Mary and was running through the house looking for little Harry.

Irene took Mama's hand and said. "Sit down here Mama. I will find him". Alice obeyed Irene like a child. Irene hurried to find Harry. She hoped that he was close. If it thundered again Mama would scream and run again. She found Harry in the Laundry room. He was sitting on the floor playing with some clothespins. She grabbed him by the hand, and took him back to where Mama was sitting. By now Mama was crying.

Irene said "Mama" remember what Daddy said. Give Mary to me and you can go to the basement".

"But what about the children"

"I will play with the children Mama. Just go and do as Daddy asked. Please Mama go".

Like a child, Alice got up from her chair, and headed for the basement. Irene and the children went to the laundry room. Irene worried about her mother down there in the basement all alone. It seemed that the storm lasted for hours. Once when the thunder got very loud Harry and Jean started to cry. Harry said "I want my Mama".

"No you don't .Mama is busy crying. Just stay here with us a little bit longer. When the storm is over, Mama will come up here with us". She picked little Harry up on her lap, and hugged him tightly to her. "Mama has to worry with the storm. We can play a game. She tapped her fingers on the table singing "where is thumb kin where is thumb kin. Here I am Here I am. How are you today sir, very well I say sir? Run away Run away".

Harry forgot he was crying and listened as Irene singing nursery rhyme songs to him. Soon the storm was over. Alice came up from the cellar. It seemed that she had forgotten about the children while she was in the basement.

"Mama, are you alright?"

"Yes Irene I think I am. I think your father was right. I get so worried about you kids, that I can't control myself. I got to the basement, and at first I wanted to run back here and force you children to go down there with me. Then I remembered what your daddy said. I knew I would have to argue with you, and I knew you would be right, because you were obeying your father. Then I heard little Harry cry for me and I started up the steps. I heard your calm voice calming him down. You sang to him. I knew you children were alright, and it calmed me down. Irene, I feel so inadequate. I went to the basement and cried and you stayed calm and calmed my children. But I think maybe we will be able to lick this thing someday.

Irene was glad when school was out for the summer. Mama told her that maybe she could learn to ride old Bessie. She liked to run around in the yard with Fuzzy, and there was one tree that Daddy said she could climb if she was very careful. She liked playing with Audrey and Jean in their playhouse in the barn. Sometimes Mama would let them take their lunch to the playhouse, and they would pretend that they were having a big party.

The summer months were beautiful in this part of the country. The children could play in their cute little play house. They made cradles for their dolls out of shoe boxes. Alice helped them to make bedclothes for their cradles. They would play for hours. Sometimes when Alice had not seen any of them for awhile, she would ring the bell. They would all come running. She would help them to make sandwiches, and they would take the sandwiches and some water, and go to their play house and have a tea party.

Harry found an old ice cream maker in Mabel's garage He asked her if it was any good and she said it had not been used for several years but she thought it was still in good shape. . Harry got it out and cleaned it up. He checked to be sure all the parts were there. It looked like it was in pretty good shape. He thought it would be so nice to surprise Irene on her birthday with cake and Ice cream.

When they got up on Saturday morning Harry told Alice that he was going to get ice to make ice cream. He asked her to make a birthday cake. She told him she would have the cake ready before he had the ice cream. He went to the ice house and got a ten pound block of ice. He brought it home and put it in a gunny sack and slammed it onto the concrete sidewalk a few times to bust it up. Then he took a hammer and beat that poor block of ice until it fell apart. Ice cream is made with just a few essentials but everybody loves ice cream

Alice and Mabel put the ingredients together using fresh eggs from the henhouse, and milk and cream from Aunt Mabel's cow some sugar and some fresh strawberries from their patch in the garden. The kids could crank it while it was still easy to turn. All the children took a turn. They were all excited. It seemed like they had cranked forever. Most thought someone must have done something wrong. Maybe they would never have Ice cream. But finally they did.

Alice brought out the cake and all sang Happy Birthday to Irene. They had a great time playing games and eating cake and ice cream. At the end of the day Irene said "Daddy, thank you for my wonderful birthday party. Often that summer some of the aunts and uncles would bring their children to visit. All the little girls enjoyed playing in the play house with the dollies.

One day Harry took several of the children to the pond to fish. There was Irene, Audrey, Jean, and their cousins, Albert, Peggy, Betty Lou and Jiggs. They went out beside the barn, and Harry dug up dirt, and the children picked up a dozen or so worms. Harry found a stick for each of them. He put some line and a hook on each one. He gave each of them a 'pole', and showed them how to put the worm on the hook. They sat there on the bank of the pond trying to catch a fish. Harry knew there were no fish in that pond. But the kids didn't. They fished for nearly an hour before starting to complain.

Finally Harry said, "It looks like the fish aren't biting today. Maybe we can come again some other time"

They picked up their things and went back to the house. But each had a fish tale to tell that evening. Jiggs swore that he had a bite, but Jean scared the fish off when she sneezed. Albert said he saw a really big one. But he must have had the wrong kind of worm. The adults listened to their stories, and laughed at each of them. No one ever told the children that there were no fish in that pond. They spent many hours fishing in that pond that summer, but no one ever caught anything. It was years later when they learned that they had been fishing just to drown worms.

In summer there was a lot of time for the children to explore. There were plenty of cousins in the area. Harry had a two sisters and a brother who lived in the area. Alice's family lived farther away. Harry's sister Agnes had six children who were close in age to his own children. They liked to spend time with Harry's children. They liked to hang around to see if Harry would find time to go fishing with them. The children were all forbidden to go near the pond unless Harry was around. So they would all run through the fields, and play in the barn and the play house.

One day their cousin Albert, who was about eleven, and Irene piled a large pile if hay in one of the empty stables. They would go up the ladder to the hay loft, and jump down onto the pile of hay. They were having a great time. Audrey, Jean and Albert's sister Mary Kay, had been playing with their dolls in the play house. When they heard the laughter they came out to see what was happening. Seeing that it looked like fun, the three smaller girls decided to join. They had played this game for almost an hour, when Alice rang the bell. This was the signal for them to go in-doors. Each child took one last jump and started for the house. Irene and Albert were half way to the house when they heard the scream. Running back to the barn, they found that Audrey, in her haste to get in that last jump. Had jumped too soon, and missed the pile of hay. She was crying in terrible pain. Albert ran as fast as he could to the kitchen and told Alice that Audrey had fallen in the barn. When Alice got to the barn, she found all of the girls crying. Audrey was the only one who was hurt but the girls were all screaming and in tears. They were all trying to talk at once. Now Alice was a very flighty person. She never knew what to do in an emergency. It was just her nature to do the wrong thing.

When she saw that Audrey was probably seriously hurt, she picked her up, and started to run. As she ran down the road, the children all ran after her. Then all at once Irene remembered that Baby Mary was alone in the house.

"Mama" she screamed "the baby. You can't leave the baby all alone" This temporarily brought Alice to her senses. But she was still not sure what to do. She stopped, and sat Audrey on a stump. She told Irene and Albert to go get Aunt Mabel. Then she left Audrey sitting on that stump crying, and went back to the house to take care of the baby. By this time Alice was crying too. She was trying to figure out what to do. In the meantime, Audrey was sitting on the stump crying. She did not know what to do. She could not get off the stump, and no one was listening to her cries. Finally Alice came to her senses, and went back to the stump where Audrey was sitting. Picking up the child she cried and said, "Oh! Honey I am so sorry. I don't know what to do with you. Aunt Mabel will be here soon. She will know what to do. You can't try to walk. I'll carry you"… She took Audrey into the house, and laid her on the couch. She sat beside her daughter and cried with her as the other children stood watching. Audrey's feet had swollen badly and were now turning blue. Alice knew that her child was in terrible pain. All she could do was to hold her child, cry and pray. If only she had a telephone. If only Harry were here. If only they lived closer to town where she could get some help. If only if only "Oh! God!" she prayed. "Please help me to help my little girl."

After what seemed like hours, Irene and Albert came back with Mabel. "Oh Mabel" Alice cried. "Help us. She fell out of the hay loft. I don't know how badly she is hurt. We need Ed. I didn't even think to tell the kids to ask you to call him. I don't know why I get so excited.

I am worthless. Even if I know what to do, I forget everything if something happens. What can we do Mabel?

"First of all" said Mabel. "You have got to get hold of yourself. You are making the child hurt worse by carrying on like this. She is hurt, but she is not going to die. You are scaring her by your actions. You need to calm yourself down. There is no way you can calm down the child if you are going crazy. I have told you before. Stop and think. When you act like this you scare the poor kids to death. From what Irene said, they were jumping on a pile of hay, and she must have missed the hay and fell to the floor. I think only her feet and legs are hurt. It looks like she may have broken something. Get some cold water, and put her feet in some cold water. Give her half of an aspirin. I already called Ed. He is on his way."

"I knew Harry should not have fixed the barn for them to play. I can't see them when they are there. Sometimes I think Harry has never grown up himself. He does such crazy things sometimes. I don't know why he doesn't think about these things before he does some of the things he does."

Speaking to the children Mabel said "You kids go on outdoors and play. Audrey will be okay. She won't be running or jumping for awhile, but I am sure she will be ok." Then to Alice she said "Alice, sometimes I think it is you, who needs to stop and think. I know you think you can't help it, but you must learn to stop and think when something like this happens. No matter whether kids are playing in the barn, or right under your feet, they can get hurt. The important thing is what you do when it does happen. Just stop and think. If you had done that, it would have been much better for Audrey. You will see, now that her feet are in the cold water, and the aspirin will be taking hold, she will not be in quite so much pain. The cold water should stop some of the swelling. Ed should be here soon and I am sure she has some broken bones. He will take care of that and make sure there are no other injuries I know that you know what should be done, but honey, you just allow yourself to get so excited, you lose all common sense."

"Yes, I do" said Alice. "But I don't know how I can control it."
"You really need to work on that" said Mabel.
"I know" said Alice.

Chapter 11

It wasn't long before Ed came. He took one look at Audrey's feet and said "My goodness child. You have broken both of your little feet. We will have to splint both of them. You will have to stay off of them for at least four weeks. That means no standing, walking, or jumping."

"It hurts so bad Uncle Ed. Can you fix it?" cried Audrey.

"I'm afraid that will take awhile sweetheart" said Ed. "I can give you a little shot this evening that will help to keep it from hurting so badly. You can go to bed and sleep for awhile. I'm sorry dear, but I am afraid is going to hurt a lot at least for a few days. There is nothing I can do about that"

"Do I have to get a shot? Shots hurt so much."

"I'm afraid so dear. It will take some of the pain away"

"Ok, but if you give me a shot, I will scream like I did the other time you gave me a shot."

"Ok just don't scream until it hurts really bad, okay. Look at your Mommy." Audrey looked at her Mother, and when she looked back, it was all over. "Look Mommy" she said. "Uncle Ed gave me a shot, and it didn't even hurt. I didn't even cry".

"You are a brave little girl sweetheart."

To Alice Ed said "she is going to be in a lot of pain for several days now I am sure. I don't think you need to worry about her injuring them farther at least until the pain goes away. You may give her half an aspirin every four hours for the pain. After the pain subsides you will

79

need to be sure she stays off those feet. These splints will hold as long as she is not too active. If they don't hold, I will have to take her to the hospital and they will put them in plaster casts. That's a long trip, and I don't think she feels up to that bumpy ride for at least a few days. I can't believe she did this."

"All I can say" said Alice "is that again I must be thankful for a doctor in the family. Ed you are certainly a blessing to us"

Ed and Mabel left and Alice sent the other children home, and told her own children they could not play in the barn any more. Irene said, "see what you did Audrey. You are so clumsy. Now we will never be able to have any fun."

"Don't start that arguing again" said Alice. "If you are going to argue I will put you to bed right now. I am tired, and I have had it for today. Why don't you read a story to the little ones?" Irene found a book and took Jean and Little Harry to the laundry room.

When Harry came home Alice lashed out at Harry blaming him because Audrey got hurt in the barn. "Oh! Alice, Sometimes I don't know what to do with you. Do you realize that when you get all nervous and upset you are a completely different person? You are not a mean person, Alice, but when you get upset, you blame everything and everybody. The kids don't know how to take you. Hell! I don't know how to take you. I wish you could hear yourself. You talk like I purposely tell the kids to do reckless things so that they can get hurt. Honey, I am teaching them to be responsible. They must be allowed to try new things. True, they should not have been jumping from the loft without an adult there. But there is no guarantee that they would not have been hurt anyway. And it was a hard lesson learned, but they did all learn a lesson today. They learned to try very hard not to hurt themselves when Daddy isn't home." Harry laughed. Alice started to cry again.

"Oh Harry." She said. "You are right. I can't handle myself in an emergency. I just fall apart. I am so afraid one of them will get hurt really seriously, and it will be my fault."

"I know honey, and we have to work on that. And they will still play in the barn. It is good for them, and it is also good for you not to have them underfoot all day, whether you know it or not. Try to have faith in yourself. Try to stop and think before you react."

"I will try. I promise."

The first few days after Audrey was hurt she was in a lot of pain. It broke Alice's heart to see her child in so much pain. Though there was very little ice in the ice-box and she knew that it must last for the rest of the week, Alice chipped off a little every few hours to put on Audrey's feet. The cool ice, kept the swelling down, therefore easing the pain. The aspirin did help some of course, but the child cried most of the day. Alice cried most of the day too. She was able to coerce the other girls to take turns playing with Audrey on the couch. Irene could read to her and they both enjoyed that for a little while, but with a short interest span, and the pain combined, it didn't really help much. They sang songs and played quiet games, but soon they ran out of things to interest Audrey. When the girls would start to argue about everything, Alice would shoo the other girls out doors. She would sing to Audrey. Alice had a beautiful voice and it was calming at least for awhile. Harry told Alice "You don't have to entertain her all the time. She should be able to color, or draw pictures. She is just crying so that you will give her your undivided attention. You always say that Mabel spoils her. You are really spoiling her now. She is not an invalid. She is a child who is temporarily handicapped. This is an opportunity for her to learn to entertain herself. She has you catering to her all the time. Alice, that is spoiling her even worse than Mabel does. Can't you see that?

"Yes I do, but I can't stand seeing her hurting so much:"

"But she is not hurting that badly now. She is feeling sorry for herself"

After the first week, the pain was not so severe. Audrey became bored with everything, she wanted to go out and play. She learned to sit on the floor, and scoot around on her butt. Without the pain, she could at least move around some. Alice worried that she would re-injure her feet.

"How would you like to make a dress for your dolly"? Alice asked. All of the girls of course wanted to learn to sew. Alice found an old work shirt of Harry's. She made a paper pattern, and showed the girls how to cut it out. Jean lost interest very soon, and decided she didn't want to learn to sew. Irene and Audrey were more interested although they got bored quickly. Audrey had a lot of trouble threading the needle, but Alice told her that she must learn to do it herself. She would cry and fret each time she ran out of thread. Alice insisted that they learn to thread needle if they wanted to learn to sew.

"I can't stop what I am doing every time you need your needle threaded. I know you can do it if you just try.

Interest waned so soon, the dress for the doll became a long drawn out process. The girls would get tired and bored easily, then they needed to do something else for awhile. Singing songs was the best pastime. They loved to sing, and Alice taught them all kinds of songs. It seemed to Alice that as long as she just sat with them and entertained them, things went smoothly, but the minute she had to do something else, the girls were bored and fretful.

"I don't know how I can stand four to six weeks of this" Alice told Harry that evening. "It has only been a little over a week and I am at my wits end. I know it is hard on Audrey to sit there day after day. It is also hard for the other girls to have to entertain her. But I just can't stop everything else to entertain them. I wasn't the one who jumped out of the hay loft but I am the one being punished."

"Honey, no one is punishing you. The kids are just bored. It is hard for kids to sit and do nothing. You know that. I'll try to spend a little more time at home with them, but I don't know that I can do as good a job of keeping them entertained. I don't even know how to sew and you know how I sing. I know how to rough and tumble, but that is out of the question now. I don't know that I can help at all. I will talk to them in the morning. I know it is hard on you. Maybe I can think of something."

Harry said "How would you like to learn to play checkers"

"Daddy" said Audrey. We don't have a checker board. You have to have a checker board and checkers to play that.

"Wanta bet? Said Harry.

He left the room for a minute and came back with a cardboard box.

"You and I can make a checker board"

"But we need checkers too"

"Don't be such a pessimist" said Harry "You are as bad as your mother"

"What in the heck is that Daddy?"

"A pessimist is someone who thinks Daddy can't make checkers"

"Audrey laughed. That isn't what it means"

He cut the side out of the box and drew a large square on the cardboard. With a ruler he blocked off sixty four blocks. "Now you can finish the checker board.

He took her red crayon and colored one block.

Then he said "Color every other block red. Skip one block and color the next.

He handed her the piece of cardboard and said. "I will be back before you are done" and he put on his hat.

"Where are you going daddy?"

"We need checkers don't we? You'll see"

He left Audrey coloring her checker box and started out. In the kitchen Alice was washing dishes. He asked her if she needed anything from town today.

She said "I thought you were going to entertain Audrey today"

"I am" he said "she is being entertained. I will be back in less than an hour. She is busy on a project we are making"

"I don't need anything today but if you think she will entertain herself for an hour, you don't know Audrey" said Alice.

"I think she will be okay until I get back. I promise I will be back as soon as I can. I'll run"

Harry ran out the door and Alice wondered what Harry was up to now. Her curiosity bothered her. She just had to know. She went into the laundry room and found Audrey very occupied in coloring.

"What are you doing?" Alice asked.

"Me and Daddy are making a checker board" she said excitedly.

"How are you going to play checkers? We don't have any checkers.

"Daddy is making the checkers" said Audrey proudly.

Alice wondered how Daddy was making checkers while he was running to town. But Audrey was happily occupied so that was fine with her. She went back to her dishes.

Meanwhile Harry hurried to town. As he was passing the cemetery Tom Peterson was just putting his mower in the car.

Tom said "Do you want a ride into town?"

"That would be great" said Harry.

They crawled into Tom's car and Tom said "You seemed to be in a hurry, is anything wrong at your house?

"No" said Harry except that my daughter broke her feet a few days ago, and she is driving my wife crazy. I am just trying to help out. This morning we are making a checker board"

Gee Whiz Harry I have a checker board we never use since the kids are grown. Why don't I just give it to you?"

Well I appreciate that Tom and maybe if you don't want it any more you might want to give it to one of my kids some day. But for now, I have her occupied making a checker board, and I think this is best for today."

"I think I see what you mean. Kid might get more fun from making it then from playing"

"You got it. Just let me out here at Charlie's. I'm gonna get the checkers here".

"Sure"

Harry ran into Charlie's and went straight to the pop machine. Sure enough, the bottle caps had not been emptied for awhile. He counted out twenty four and then grabbed a couple more just in case one gets lost. He said "Hello" to Charlie and told him that he just came into steal a few bottle caps. Then he headed straight for home.

Alice had lunch ready when Harry got home. She said "You are just on time. Go bring Audrey out here for lunch"

Harry went into the laundry room and said "Well, kitten, did you finish your part of the project?"

Almost" she said. I have one more box to fill. I fell asleep. I'm sorry daddy, I got tired".

"That's ok sweetheart. I wouldn't want you to get too tired. Mama has lunch ready. Let's go eat lunch before we finish". He carried her to the kitchen.

After lunch they went back to the laundry room. Audrey quickly finished coloring the last square of the board. Then Harry handed her twelve of the bottle cap lids. He proceeded to put his 'checkers' upside down. He told her she should place hers right side up. That way they would know who's they were. He explained to her how to play. By the time they had played for an hour, Audrey was tired of the game. But he knew that she would have another way to occupy herself.

The next day when Harry was talking to Mabel He told her about the problem Alice was having with the girls. Mabel said she didn't have any answers, but she did have a couple of card games. Maybe if Harry could teach them to play cards, that would keep them occupied for awhile. She gave him a deck of Old Maid cards, and a deck of Authors. Harry went home to teach his daughters how to play Old Maid. He had a hard time explaining to the girls that all of them could not win. "Somebody has to lose" he told them. "The game would not be any fun if you won every game. The purpose of the game is not to win all the time, but to play and have fun."

"But it is more fun to win" said Audrey.

"When you know how to be a good loser, it is even fun when you lose. "

"If you play real nice, and don't bother Mommy so much for a few

85

more days, I will hitch Bessie to the buggy, and take you to Aunt Mabel's on Saturday. How would you like that?"

"Okay Daddy, we will try."

And the girls did try. They played cards, sewed some on their doll dresses, and tried to entertain each other. But when Irene got bored she would go out doors for awhile and when Audrey was left alone, it all started over again.

On Saturday, true to his word, Harry hitched up the buggy and took the children to Mabel's. This gave Alice a break. She wished she could just lie down and take a nap. The house was so quiet. There were no children bickering. Oh! How she enjoyed the peace and quiet. But she could not rest. She was three days behind on her work. She had a dress to finish for Mrs. Clary, and she needed to clean the windows in the front of the house before the Kinney's came home next weekend.

Tending the children had become such a chore recently. Alice usually loved taking care of her children. Audrey was so impatient. Now that she was not in so much pain, she wanted to get up and go. It was getting hard to keep her off her feet. It had been just about ten days since this had happened. That meant that she must stay off her feet for at least two or three more weeks. Alice didn't know how she could do it. Irene was tired of sitting with Audrey. They were always bickering. Alice knew that she could not neglect her own work much longer. She was working at her sewing, but the longer she thought about her circumstances the more helpless she felt. As she became more and more depressed, she began to cry. With tears filling her eyes it became impossible for her to see to sew. She grabbed her mop and bucket and went to the front of the house.

She accomplished a lot of work that afternoon. As she cried harder, she worked harder. She had done more work in four hours than she usually did in a day. But she was totally exhausted. When Harry came home that evening he came without Audrey.

"Mabel said she will take her off your hands for a few days. She said she has nothing pressing for this week."

"You should not have left her there. Mabel will just spoil her more. She will probably be less contented when she comes back home".

"Well I am sure she will be ill tempered and discontented wherever she is for a couple of weeks. And I know that you are worried about the work you have been letting go while you try to keep her entertained. Now you will have time to catch up on some of it".

"I have already done that" said Alice. "All I have left to do is to hem Mrs. Clary's dress. And of course there is some work to be done in the garden. But you are going to do that tomorrow".

"Oh! I am?" joked Harry. "And when did we decide that?"

"I decided that when I had so much 'free' time today". She answered.

While Audrey was at Mabel's things went more smoothly for Alice. She was able to catch up on her sewing, and even make a dress for Irene from a dress that Mabel had given her. Alice had already cut down as many of her own dresses as she could afford to do without. Harry also lost some clothing. Little Harry was outgrowing his clothes so Alice cut down a pair of Harry's pants. She was able to make little Harry two pairs from one pair of Harry's.

It was harvest time, and Harry spent a lot of time at home with Alice. They preserved as much food as they could in preparation for the winter. If this winter was as hard as the last, they needed to be prepared for it. They would work from sunup to sundown picking, cleaning, preparing and canning. Sometimes they worked until the wee hours of the morning.

The children had learned to entertain themselves most of the time. Irene even entertained the little ones for hours each day, calling Alice from the field only when she was really needed. Irene had become a regular little mother for the younger children. She diapered the babies and fed them, sang and rocked them to sleep. Everyone had a job to do. Even the younger children helped by carrying and fetching. It was hard work for everyone, but the family worked together all day, and when night came they all fell exhausted into bed.

Audrey spent three weeks at Mabel's. Mabel knew that Audrey would be better off with her. The child was a real handful. Mabel had a lot of patience, but she lost it often during those three weeks. She did everything she could to please the child, but Audrey was discontented. After the pain was gone, Audrey still cried a lot. She cried about everything. Mabel finally lost her temper one day.

"Okay!" she said to Audrey. "Here is what we are going to do. From now on, if you cry for nothing, I am going to walk out of the room and I will not come back until you stop crying. I know you are bored, and I know you want to get down and play. You cannot do that. When Uncle Ed comes home this weekend, he will probably take off the splints. You probably will still not be able to walk much for a little while. But until you can, I will not be listening to all this crying over nothing. Do you understand"?

Audrey started to cry all over again. Mabel simply stood up and walked out of the room closing the door behind her. Audrey was shocked. At first she screamed. Then she stopped to listen for Mabel's return. She didn't hear a sound. She called "Aunt Mabel". But she got no answer. Finally, when she realized what had actually happened, she stopped crying. She picked up her crayons and started to color. Mabel waited for about five minutes. Then she opened the door. "That's better" she said. From then on, whenever Audrey started to fuss and fret, Mabel would simply walk out and close the door. It didn't take long for Audrey to get the message.

When Ed came home that weekend he took off the splints. When Audrey stood on her feet, she found that she couldn't walk without help. She started to cry. Ed explained to her that she would have to learn to walk again like little Mary was now doing, one step at a time. She had believed that when he took off the splints that she could do everything she had done before. For the next couple of days, Mabel closed the door a lot.

Finally it was time for Audrey to go back home. It would soon be time for school to start. The family was busy doing all sorts of things preparing for winter. Audrey missed the attention she had been getting from Aunt Mabel. But she soon learned that her fretting did less good here than it did with Aunt Mabel. Everyone was just too busy to listen to her. So she stopped crying and soon joined in to help.

Chapter 12

There were very few families in town that didn't seem hurt so much by the depression. But it seemed that even the people, who had once been prosperous, had lost most of their money when the banks went under. Some people like Harry, had never had a lot to start with. But it was hard on everybody. A few people had managed to save what they had, but even they were struggling. Harry's sister and her husband were one such family. Their children were nearly grown their son had a job. And of course Ed, being the only doctor for miles around, was doing alright. But almost everyone in town owed him money. They often paid him with a pound of butter or a dozen eggs.

Mabel and Ed also gave to the town as much as they could. Mabel always had jars of food for a neighbor if she knew they were hungry. Ed delivered many babies with no pay at all. Mabel always had a kind word for everyone. She did a lot of volunteer work throughout the county. When Franklin Roosevelt was inaugurated in the spring of nineteen thirty three, he implemented a relief program that was supposed to boost the economy. Mabel volunteered to be on the relief board. Everybody was hoping this relief program would help them to get through this economic slump.

Harry was one of the first in the area to sign up for the relief program. Almost everyone was shocked when Harry was turned down. He was not eligible at that time. Of course Harry blamed politics. He believed that he had been turned down because he was a republican and had not even voted for FDR. Mabel tried to reassure him that was not the reason, but Harry could not believe that he was not eligible. If this program was not created for people like him, then who was it for.

He felt like a failure all over again when he had to tell Alice that they would not get any of this money either. "It just doesn't seem fair" he told her. "I work as hard as I can, and it seems that when I take one step forward I slide back two. I was just hoping that this was the light at the end of the tunnel. But it looks like it is just another black hole. I don't care for myself, but you and the kids deserve so much more that I can give you."

"Harry" Alice said. "The kids are not really going hungry. They don't have the best, and I would like to see them getting more meat, and fruit especially, but I don't think 'coffee soup' for breakfast now and then will really stunt their growth forever."

"Coffee soup?" asked Harry.

"Well when we don't have much for breakfast, I take a little bread, break it into a bowl, and pour a little coffee with a lot of sugar and milk on it." It fills their stomachs and they like it. I only give them that once or twice a week. I don't think it will hurt them."

"I doubt it will hurt them, but it can't be very good for them either."

"Let's not worry about little things like that" she told him. "But think about it this way. If the government says that we are not eligible for this relief, or what ever they call it. That means that there are a lot of other people who are worse off than we are, at least according to the United States Government. If they are, then God help them. Maybe this relief will help them. And maybe, just maybe, if the government helps them, it will make it easier somehow for us to help ourselves. We will make it through this Harry, I am sure we will."

It seemed that when Harry fell into a depression for a few days. Alice was able to bring him back into focus. Then a week or so later it was Harry's turn to do the same for Alice.

"The thing I hate most is the way our kids are ridiculed at school.

I know that a lot of the other children are not much better off than ours, but I think there are a couple of kids who are so jealous of our kids that they are really making life miserable for them at school."

"Why would they be jealous of our kids? They sure don't have anything to be jealous over" said Harry.

"Oh yes they do. They live in a great big beautiful house. The children don't realize that it is not ours. Some of them think we must be rich. Anyone living it a palace must be rich. I know that all the adults in town know we are as poor as church mice, but to children the world looks a lot different. They dress nice and they are the doctor's nieces."

"Do you really think that is true? Children are jealous of our kids because we live here?"

I think that has something to do with it. I really don't know, but Audrey came home the other day and said Florence Richards had all the kids calling her four eyes. Do you realize our little girl is the only child in that whole school who wears glasses? She probably looks like a freak to those kids" Alice said.

"But don't they know people wear glasses because they don't see well. That is no reason for ridicule" said Harry. "Children can be so mean.

"I'm sure she will learn to live with it, but I feel so sorry for her. All I can do is tell her, "Don't pay any attention. They are jealous. That's no answer for a six year old."

One day it all came to a head. Alice had made a suit for Mrs. Richards. When Mrs. Richards had picked it up, she had brought a box of clothing which her children had out grown. She said "My children have outgrown these things and I thought you could get some use from them. I am sure there is a lot more wear in them, but my kids are growing so fast they are coming out of their clothes"

Alice had accepted the box and thanked her for it. Usually Alice would use hand-me-downs for doll clothes. Or she would alter them in some way that the child who had worn them would not immediately recognize them.

There were a couple of really nice things in that box, and Alice thought they would look so nice on her children that she kept them as they were. Too late she realized that had been a mistake. One day Irene and Audrey had both worn a dress that had come from that box. Florence was in a particularly arrogant mood that day.

At recess, she started to ridicule Irene. "You even have to wear my old clothes" she said. "Don't you have anything else to wear?" "Your sister is a four eyed hog" she said. "Why don't you run up to Auntie Mabel's and tell her all the kids are picking on you?"

Audrey went to the teacher and told her. The teacher sent Audrey to her desk. Then she went out to ring the bell and bring in all the children. The teacher did not rebuke the children for teasing, but acted as though nothing had happened. She was hoping that it would be forgotten. The teacher honestly thought that this was the best way to handle the situation. If you don't mention it, it will go away. Irene was very angry. When school was out that evening Irene took Audrey by the hand and said "Come on, I need you to help me." She hurried down the street and pulled Audrey behind a large tree by the post office. She whispered into Audrey's ear. They waited quietly until Florence got close to the tree. Then they pounced. The element of surprise was on their side. Florence was two years older than Irene. She was much bigger than either of them, but there were two of them. By the time Florence knew what was happening, she had a bloody knee, her clothing was all torn, she had a lot of bruises, and she was crying. As soon as she was able, she took off running for home as fast as she could go. Irene and Audrey just stood, smiling, as they watched her go. Then they turned and walked home.

They immediately told Alice what they had done. Irene knew that she was never to start a fight. Her father had told her that if someone hurt her, she should defend herself, but if he ever learned that she had started a fight, she would be punished. She wanted her mother to know what had provoked her hoping to have her mother on her side when the fireworks came. She was almost surprised when her mother

NYDA A. WRIGHTSMAN

punished her. "I want you to go to your room until your father comes home" she said "you too Audrey. You know we do not want you fighting like cats and dogs. There are better ways to settle arguments than with fists."

"I don't care Mother, I can't take it anymore. She was teasing Audrey, and just picking and picking. I couldn't stand it any more. And the teacher didn't even yell at her. I will never wear that dress again. You can't make me."

"Me neither, Mama, Florence is a mean and hateful girl, and I hate her."

"No, you don't hate her" said Alice. "You may dislike her, but never never hate anyone."

"I don't care" said Audrey again. "I hate her anyway."

"Go to your room" said their mother again, and the two girls stomped up the stairs.

Alice stood in the kitchen getting angrier by the minute. This hateful girl was making life miserable for her girls, and she would not stand for it. She found a box, gathered up all the things that had been in the box that was given to her, closed the box and waited for her husband to come home. When Harry got home Alice told him that she had an errand to run. Picking up the box she started out the door. "I will be back soon" she said. And without another word, she was gone. It was about a two mile walk to town and with each step she took she became a little angrier. Alice had a wicked temper and she wanted to strangle someone. She did not know what she would say to Mrs. Richards. She was going over and over in her head just what she wanted to say to this woman.

Her temper was just about at the boiling point, when she reached the Richards porch. She knocked on the door. When the door opened, Mrs. Richards started to greet her. Alice didn't allow her to say a word, she started in.

"I guess you know what happened after school today" she said, "at least you know Florence's side of it. I want you to know that I am punishing my girls, but even though I can't tell them, I have never been more proud of them. Your daughter is a snotty spoiled brat who needs some lessons in humanity. She has been making life miserable for my children since they started to school." Mrs. Richards tried to say something several times but Alice kept going. "For some reason or other she has it in for my girls, and there is no excuse for a girl as big as yours to pick on little girls. Now she has some of the others laughing at them because they seem to like to see little girls cry. The same 'tailor' who makes your 'tailor made' clothes makes terrible looking 'home made' clothes for my daughters. Well find yourself a new 'tailor'. I have made the last one for you"

When the other woman tried to protest Alice went on. "And as for that box, as far as I am concerned, you may wipe your behind on that stuff. We don't need it, or want it" And with that she turned and started back the way she had come. From that day forward Alice's daughters never wore a hand-me-down unless it had been disguised in some way. She was determined that this would never happen to her girls again.

When she returned home she told Harry about the day's events. He was shocked that she had told Mrs. Richards that she would not make any more clothes for her. That woman was her best customer. But Harry always did say that Alice didn't charge her enough. He told Alice that she needed to start charging at least a dollar for each garment. He explained to Alice that her time was valuable, and she didn't charge enough for it. Alice was afraid that if she charged more, people would not have her to do the work. Harry told her that she could live without Mrs. Richards as a customer. He said that she was a snooty old lady who wanted everything for nothing, and that Alice had been a fool to do so much for so little anyway. As the next few weeks went by, Alice had more orders for clothing than she had ever had. It seemed that as word got around that she had told the old lady what she thought of her, people found a new respect for Alice's work.

Now it seemed that Alice had all the orders she could handle. The problem was that she could not find time to do everything she wanted to do. There was always a project on her sewing table and she often stayed up sewing until the wee hours of the morning.

Chapter 13

That autumn Harry and Alice had two children in school. The school in Elkton was a little two room school house. First, second and third grade had a lady teacher. Her name was Miss Flannigan. Mr. Titus was the teacher in the fourth, fifth and sixth grade. He was also the principal. If the children were to be punished it was Mr. Titus who generally did it. Irene was now in the fourth grade. Audrey was in the first.

The weather was still beautiful. Most afternoons it was just a nice walk home through the woods. The girls were not afraid to walk through the woods. They wanted to take advantage of the nice weather because they knew that in a few months the snow would block the road, and they would again have to walk through the cemetery just as it was starting to get dark. It was kind of scary. There were a lot of shadows at that time in the evening making it scary. Daddy had explained to them that the people in the cemetery were all dead, and that they could not hurt them. They knew that. But it was scary all the same.

When the snow came, and the wind blew hard, there was one place on the road toward their house that always drifted shut. The snow piled over their heads and in order to get around that spot, they must go through the cemetery. Daddy had showed them where their grandparents were buried. They felt safer walking past those graves.

They were sure their grandparents wouldn't harm them. Once

they got past the grandparent's graves, it was only a few steps to the fence, and once over the fence they would run like the dickens to the house. If Harry was able he would usually wait for them at the cemetery, and walk home with them because he knew it was a little frightening for them. They were really frightened sometimes, but they didn't want to tell their dad. He thought they were such brave little girls.

In mid winter, when the weather was really snowy and the wind was blowing hard, they would stop at Mabel's. Their dad would sometimes let them stay there, and he would bring them clean clothes the next morning. One Friday evening, just after the first real snow of the season they had stopped at Mabel's. She told them that their dad had gone on home and they were to go too. The snow had stopped, and since there was no school next day, they should go on home. They left immediately because it was nearly dark. They knew it would be dusk when they reached the cemetery. They hurried along, hoping that Dad would be waiting.

"If Daddy stopped at Aunt Mabel's, that means he is at home. So he will probably meet us at the cemetery" said Irene.

"I hope so" said Audrey. "Sometimes I am so scared, aren't you Irene?"

"Yes, but don't tell Daddy. I try to make him think I am as brave as he thinks I am. But sometimes last year when I had to walk alone, I cried. I never told him. At least this year there will be two of us, It doesn't seem so scary when you have someone with you, I am glad you are going to be with me this year".

As they approached the cemetery they saw a figure near their grandfather's tombstone. "There's Daddy" said Irene, and they hurried to meet him. But it was not their daddy. A person with a bag over his head jumped from behind the tombstone. "I am going to eat you" said a voice, and he grabbed at Audrey. Irene knew that voice. It was one of the boys from school. Audrey screamed and tried to run but the boy just held her tighter. Another boy jumped from another spot and grabbed Irene. "I know who you are" said Irene. "I am going to tell on you". The boys just laughed. Audrey was crying. She screamed again. Just at that time Harry stepped out from behind another tombstone and grabbed the boys, both at once, one with each hand. He started to shake them. They were much more frightened than the girls had been, and for good reason. This man was angry. Harry held on to the boys and said "Irene pull off those bags. Let's see who these bold boys are".

As Irene removed the bags she said "I know who they are. They are the Smith boys, Tom and John. I knew Tom as soon as he spoke. They were trying to scare us Dad".

"I'm sorry Mr. Jackson" said Tom. "We were just trying to have a little fun".

"Well, let's see if I can have a little fun. I should beat you boys to within an inch of your life. If the only kind of fun you can think of, is to scare little girls. I can give you a dose of your own medicine".

Still holding the boys by the back of their coats, Harry said "Come on girls follow me." and headed back towards town. He marched straight up to the door of the Smith house. "By then John was crying. "Dad will kill us" he said. "Please don't tell Dad". But Harry did not hear a word. When Mr. Smith opened the door, Harry said "Your boys have something to tell you, Don't you boys".

John was crying so hard he could not have talked if he wanted to and Tom was simply standing there. "Well" said their dad, "What have you done now"?

"We weren't going to hurt them" said Tom "We just wanted to have a little fun"

"What did you do?" He asked.

The boys did not say a word. They knew that their dad would be angry. They also knew that Harry would tell their dad if they did not answer. But they just stood there.

"What did they do Mr. Jackson?" said Mr. Smith.

"I think they would rather tell you themselves, wouldn't you boys?"

The boys just stood there shaking their heads.

"Harry gave each of the boys a little shake and said "Now boys, tell your Dad what you did.

"We hid in the cemetery to scare the girls. We weren't going to hurt them. I swear Dad, We didn't mean any harm".

"Go to your room right now. I will tend to you later". Then to Harry he said, "Those boys will be punished for this. They have been in quite a lot of mischief lately. I don't know where they get these ideas but I will see that this doesn't happen again".

"I will appreciate that" said Harry. "When the snow drifts and the road closed, it is necessary for the girls to walk through the cemetery. I know that they are a little frightened, but I have told them that nothing will hurt them there. I am determined that nothing will. These boys can have their fun somewhere else.

"They didn't scare me" said Irene "but Audrey didn't know who they were. She is only in second grade, so she is in the other room".

"Whether they scared you or not, that was a nasty thing to do, and if my boys have to find their jolly's scaring babies it is time for some serious punishment".

"I'm not a baby" said Irene.

"Of course you aren't. I didn't mean you, they scared your little sister, and she is not much more than a baby."

"I just want to see that it doesn't happen again" said Harry

"I can pretty much guarantee that" said Mr. Smith.

With that Harry took his daughters by the hand, and they walked back trough the cemetery toward their home. They played a little game along the way. He would ask Audrey how much is two and six. Then he would say Irene what is four times eight. He expected an immediate answer. If they had to think for too long he would ask another question and completely confuse them. They liked to play games with their dad and he was always making up games to help them with their homework. Harry had only gone to school as far as the sixth grade because Elkton had no higher grades. To go to the higher grades he would have had to go on the train, and his father could not afford that. Harry went to the sixth grade for three years because his father said that "An idle mind is the devils workshop". His father made him go to school until he was sixteen.

By the time the girls got home and started to tell Alice of their experience, they thought it was rather funny. "Daddy grabbed those boys both at the same time. They had tried to scare us, but he scared them even more. It turned out to be so funny. But I wouldn't want to be those boys tonight. Mr. Smith was really mad".

"I'm glad it turned out okay" said Alice. "Come on and eat. Your supper is getting cold."

The next morning at about ten thirty, there was a knock on the door. Irene opened the door, and there stood the Smith boys. Tom said "Is your dad here?"

"Daddy" Irene called. "Somebody wants to talk to you".

"Harry came into the kitchen and was shocked to see the two boys from the day before. "Hello, boys" he said. What can I do for you?"

"That is supposed to be our question" said Tom. "Dad said that we are to work as slaves for you for at least two days. He said if you can't find anything for us to do, we are to spend the next two days chopping wood for you".

Harry could not keep from laughing. "I'm sorry boys. But I do find that rather funny. I believe that if you were my boys I would have probably thought of the same sort of punishment. But I will tell you what. Chopping wood for two days would be real slave labor, and I don't believe in slavery. But I agree with your father that you need punished. I have to shovel the drift out of the road so that the girls don't have to walk through the cemetery next week. I think that will be about a two day job for two boys such as you. If you will come with me I will find a couple of shovels in the shed out there. If you come in at around twelve thirty, my wife will have a sandwich and some milk for your lunch It is pretty cold out there so if you get really cold, you may take a ten minute break every hour or so. We really don't believe in slave labor".

Thank you Mr. Jackson" said Tom. They went with Harry to the shed to get the shovels.

When Harry came back in to the house the girls were laughing. They thought it was rather funny that the boy's dad had made them come to work for their dad. And to think that they had to shovel snow was especially amusing. They were surprised that their Dad was angry at them. "Laughing at someone else's punishment isn't much nicer that trying to scare someone just for the fun of it. I do not want to see you laughing about this to anyone else. And if I hear that you have told the other kids at school, you will be punished worse than those boys are being punished today. And don't you forget it.

That took the fun away from the whole thing. Now they were not even allowed to tell the other kids about this.

Chapter 14

In school the children ridiculed Audrey a lot about her glasses. One day Joey Barkley grabbed her glasses and ran with them. He threatened to throw them down in the out-house. Audrey thought he was just mean enough to do that. She ran after him but he was much bigger then she was and ran much faster. He was always a step ahead of her. She picked up a rock and threw it at him. It didn't hit him, but came close enough to threaten him. Joey threw her glasses at her. She threw another rock. It managed to hit him right above his left eye. She picked up her glasses and put them on. She did not say another word to him. She had her glasses back, and she thought that should be the end of it. But Joey ran to the teacher He told the teacher that Audrey threw a rock at him. He was bleeding just enough that the teacher knew he was telling the truth…

Mr. Titus called Audrey from the playground. "You may not go outdoors for recess for the rest of the week" he told her.

"But" Audrey tried to protest but the teacher did not want to hear about it. He told her to shut up and go to her seat.

"But Mr. Titus" Audrey began again.

"No!" he said "go to your seat"

"Can I tell you why" she said

"Not another word young lady" Mr. Titus said. "After school is out this evening you will stay until all the other children are gone. I will take you home to your Dad. He will be informed what a hateful little girl you have been today"

Audrey sat in her seat and cried all afternoon. Both teachers told their class what a naughty little girl Audrey was. She was not allowed to say anything. She just sat and cried.

When school was out that evening, Mr. Titus took Audrey by the hand, and took her home. He told Harry that Audrey had hit Joey in the head with a rock. Harry was very upset with his daughter. .

"But Daddy" Audrey said, "Joey grabbed my glasses and he ran away with them. He said he was going to throw them down in the outhouse. Then when I threw the rock he threw them at me. They landed on the sidewalk. I thought they were broken, so I threw another rock. That one hit him. And I don't care"

"Is this true?" Harry asked the teacher.

"I was never informed about that" said the teacher.

"I tried to tell you. You told me to shut up and sit down. So I did"

"Is that true?" said Harry

"I guess it is", said Mr. Titus. "But throwing rocks is against the rules at school".

"I would think throwing someone's glasses down the toilet should be against the rules too" said Harry.

"But come on Audrey. You are going to go and apologize to Joey for throwing a rock at him"

"No! I'm not" said Audrey.

"Yes you will" said her father, and taking her by the hand he led her towards town.

"Daddy" Audrey said. "You will have to punish me"

"Yes, but first you will apologize to Joey".

"No I won't"

By this time they were standing on the Barkley's front porch. Joey and his mother stood in the doorway.

"Joey" said Audrey. "My Daddy says that I have to apologize to you. But I am going to be punished either way. I will not apologize to you because I am not sorry. My Daddy will punish me if I lie anyway.

So I am not going to apologize because that would be a lie. I am not sorry. I wish I had hit you harder". And with that she turned to her Dad and said. "Okay, now you can punish me".

As they walked home that evening Audrey said to her Dad "Are you going to spank me Daddy?"

"Do you think I should?

"Well. I don't know, but I would rather have a spanking for hitting Joey with a rock than for lying, and you know I would be lying if I said I was sorry".

I will have to think about this for awhile.

That evening after the children had gone to sleep Harry said. "I don't know about Audrey: She is so uncompromising at times".

"I think she is a lot like you dear I'll bet you would have done the same when you were a kid. I can almost hear you now".

"I think you might be right. But I do have to punish her. I just don't know how".

"Don't ask me" said Alice. "I have no idea".

The next day Harry called Audrey to him. He said "We have to talk about what you did yesterday".

"Yes Sir" Audrey said.

"You know I have to punish you for hitting Joey with a rock".

"Yes Daddy, I know, but I am not sorry so I won't apologize"

"Then I guess we are at a stalemate"

"What does that mean?"

"It means that we are deadlocked. You do not think you did wrong, but I must punish you anyway.

"I know it was wrong to hit Joey with the rock, Daddy".

"Then why do you think you should not be punished?"

"I didn't say I shouldn't be punished Daddy. I know I will be punished. But I still will not apologize. Joey didn't have to apologize to me for taking my glasses and threatening to throw them down the toilet. He didn't even admit that he did it. And he is not being punished is he?"

"I don't know dear, but he is not my child, you are. Are you saying that if Joey would apologize to you, that you would apologize to him?"

"I haven't really thought about that, but it might make it a little more even. I think he should be punished too. I think we should both be punished."

"I can't punish him, Audrey, he is not my child. I think if he was I might punish him too".

"Well if you are going to punish me, I hope you do it soon"

"Why?"

"Because I cried last night in bed, and I want to get it over so that I can sleep tonight".

"Okay" said her Dad. "Get your coat. We are going to settle this once and for all"

"Where are we going?"

"We are going to Joey's house".

They went to the door and Harry knocked. When Joey's mother came to the door, Harry said "Excuse me Mrs. Barkley but may we have a word with Joey please?"

Mrs. Barkley called for Joey and he came into the room. Harry could see that he had a guilty look on his face. He seemed to be afraid of something.

"Sonny" said Harry. "When you told your teacher that Audrey hit you with a rock, why did you not tell him why she did that?"

"He didn't ask" said Joey.

"Have you told your mother why she hit you with a rock?"

Speaking to Joey's mother Harry said "Didn't you ask him why this little girl had hit him with a rock?"

"I didn't even think any more about it. He wasn't hurt" she said.

"No" said Joey.

"Okay, Joey" Harry said. "I am asking. Why did Audrey hit you with a rock?"

"Didn't she tell you?'

"I'm asking you".

"Okay! I took her glasses and ran away with them"

"What did you tell her you were going to do with them?

I wasn't gonna throw them down the out-house. I was just teasing her"

"Joey Barkley" his mother yelled. "Did you threaten to throw this little girl's glasses down the toilet?"

"I wasn't gonna do it Mom. I was just teasing"

"Joey" I want you to apologize to this little girl, and I want you to promise me that you will never do anything like that again, to her of anyone else".

"I'm sorry. I was only teasing".

"I wasn't going to throw do it anyway.

"Audrey I am so sorry that my son did such an awful thing to you. I know that even having to wear those glasses makes you feel sometimes like you are being punished. And when the other children are nasty about it you feel even worse. I am so sorry. And Joey, do you have any idea how much money goes into a pair of glasses"

"I wasn't gonna throw them down the toilet".

Well you threw them at me the sidewalk is bricks. You could have broke them.

"Okay" said Harry. Let's not start the civil war again. We will all forgive each other and everything will be ok.

In the winter the children often played in the laundry room. There was a cot and a couple of chairs there. They could use the table for coloring, or reading. Audrey and Irene often did their homework there. When Alice was working in the kitchen she could glance in occasionally to see what was going on.

One such evening, Audrey was lying on the cot sleeping. Jean was sitting at the table with a celluloid pen in her hand. She reached up, and held the pen over the light coming from the kerosene lamp on the table. The pen caught fire. Seeing the fire, Jean threw the pen. It landed in Audrey's hair. Immediately Audrey's hair was in flames. The collar of her dress was starting to burn. Both girls screamed. Harry came running. He took one look at the situation and grabbed Audrey up and started to beat the fire out with his hands. He grabbed the blanket from the cot and wrapped it around her. Audrey kept yelling "Don't whip me Daddy, I didn't do it". She didn't realize her father was putting out the fire. She was not burned badly. The hair on one side of her head, and nearly all of the back had been burned off. She a few burns on her neck and shoulders. When Harry realized what had happened he grabbed Jean up, and spanked her bottom. He said "You know better than to play with fire. You could have set the house on fire. We could have all been killed, don't ever do such a foolish thing again".

Again poor Audrey had been hurt, but this time it was not by her own foolishness, but by someone else's. But this time she was a little older. She was a little braver. And she was at least able to get around. Alice worried about infection. A burn can get infected so easily, and children don't understand anything about why parents worry so much. Alice took an old white sheet. She made several little white bonnets for Audrey to wear over the bandages on her head. They were really very cute hats, and Audrey looked nice with them, but she was afraid the other children at school would laugh at her. The first morning that Jean was to go to school after this happened; Alice dressed the smaller children and took them all to Mabel's. She left the children with Mabel and went to the school. She explained to the teacher, and to the students that Audrey had been burned, and that this was necessary. She told the children that Audrey did not need pity. But that she was afraid they would laugh at her for wearing that little hat. She asked them to please refrain from laughing at her daughter.

After Alice left, the teacher told her class, that if she heard of any one laughing at Audrey's hat, they would be punished. There was no problem. In fact everybody thought the little hats that Audrey wore were rather cute. Audrey wore those little hats for a couple of months until the bandages could all come off, and then until some of her hair grew back. Alice had cut all the hair off so that it would grow back evenly, so Audrey needed to wear the hats until it grew back. Later when the hats were no longer necessary, one of the girls told Audrey "We really liked your hats. They looked nice on you but some of the kids probably would have laughed, but they were told they better not."

"I have learned that. there are some kids who just like to make others miserable. I know that I will never make fun of anyone again. My dad says that making fun of any one is just petty and mean. He said that there are some people who would laugh if a blind man fell over a rock. But there are other people who would move the rock so that he wouldn't do it again. I want to be the one who moves the rock"

"I like your dad" said the other girl.

Chapter 15

Just before Christmas Harry found out about the new work program that president Roosevelt had implemented in order to put people to work. It was supposed to help to boost the economy be giving people a paycheck. Harry signed on to work for WPA. Works Progress Administration (Later named Work Projects Administration)

He would work thirty hours a week, and be paid twenty dollars a month. The government was building new roads. Cars were becoming a popular means of travel. Roads were needed to accommodate them. Most of the people who had been on relief for months were forced to go to work to earn this relief check. Harry had not been eligible for the relief program, but he was eligible for the work program. For the first time in nearly two and a half years, Harry had a real paying job. His first paycheck had to be spent on some decent work clothes. It was winter, and he was outside in the bitter cold all day. He had to get at least a pair of work shoes, and some kind of warm clothing. He would leave the house every morning with several layers of clothing. But by the time evening came, he was chilled to the bone. He could not afford to get sick. Alice insisted that he take that first check and get himself some clothes. As much as he hated himself for spending what little money he had, on himself, he did just that. It felt good to be able to go to work. Now it felt better to go to work and not freeze all day long. But it did not feel good to know that his children could have had a nice Christmas with that money. Even though Harry knew it was the right thing to do, he felt bad to know that there would not be another check before Christmas. That meant another Christmas with nothing for the children.

This one would be worse than the last. Last year Alice had cut down her own clothes to make things for the girls. This year she had none left to use. Last year he had made furniture and Alice had made dolls and doll clothes. This year the materials had all been used up. Last year they had very little. This year they had nothing. Even though he was now working, there was still no money. But things were looking up. They would survive this. They still had each other, and how he loved his little family. He would have done anything for them. There was only so much he could do.

Joe and Marge came the next afternoon. When Marge saw the house she said "Oh it is so nice to see the place looking like this. It looks like it did when Mama was here. I do love this house Joe"

"I know you do dear" said Joe. "Do you think we should give Alice a little extra for Christmas this year? She had to have spent a lot of time on this place? I haven't seen it this clean since we moved out"

"It never has been this clean since we moved" Marge said. "Yes I think she deserves a bonus. I think we can give her about ten dollars. We would have paid the cleaning crew that much and they didn't do nearly as nice a job as Alice has done".

Joe knocked on Alice's door. He introduced Marge to Alice and Harry. They commented on how nice the place looked. Marge told Alice that no one had ever cleaned that house like that except her mother. When Joe handed Alice the ten dollars he said "Marge said she thought you should have a bonus. We are very happy with your work. The house has not looked so good for years".

"I don't know what to say, except Thank you I wasn't expecting this, but it is really nice".

Mabel told Alice one day, "I know how hard you worked last year to make Christmas for those kids. They believed it was the greatest Christmas ever. Now I know that this year will be even worse. Ed and

I have decided that we can help a little. I know that the girls would like some china for their little cupboard Harry made last year. I found a set the last time I was in Cumberland. It was really a beautiful little set of dishes, I bought them. They are tucked away in my chifarobe. I will find at least one nice thing for each of the children. You only need to worry about the fruit and nuts that go into the stockings. Let us handle the rest. It won't be much, but it will be enough. Don't worry Alice. Things are looking up for all of us. They say it is always darkest just before the dawn. Let's hope the dawn is coming soon"

But Joe gave me a ten dollar bonus yesterday. I was so afraid that the girls were going to have to go another winter without boots. But I think I have enough to get each of them both shoes and boots.

"Mabel. I have been expecting the dawn for what seems like an eternity. Sometimes I just about give up. And then I talk to you, and you make me feel like the whole thing is just a bad dream, and I will wake up soon.

"Maybe it is Alice. You know God doesn't give you more than he thinks you can handle".

"I know, but He must have a lot more faith in me, than I have in myself".

"Maybe you just need more faith in yourself then".

True to her word, Mabel and Ed came out late on Christmas Eve. They visited for awhile before the children went to bed. They talked about Santa. "Mama said that Santa has too many kids this year. She says we have to share" said Jean. "Do you think Santa will bring us anything?"

"I believe that Santa will bring something for every good little boy and girl. Even when times are hard, Santa finds something for everyone. He will bring you something. Sometimes he can't bring everything you want, but there will always be another Christmas. And remember, Christmas is to celebrate the baby Jesus' birthday. That is the real meaning of Christmas. So if we don't get everything we want, we need to just remember that".

"I believe it is time now for good little boys and girls to go to bed" said Alice. "Aunt Mabel, Will you read the Christmas story to them. I am sure they would like that".

"Alright, let's go" she said leading the children up the stairs. They were all in their pajamas in short order. Mabel sat in a chair in the girl's room with little Harry on her lap. The girls crawled into bed as she read. Before the story was finished they were all in dreamland. She quietly carried little Harry to his crib and tucked him in. Then she went back downstairs.

"Mission accomplished" she said. "They all have visions of sugarplums, and all that stuff. Let's do our thing Ed".

Ed and Mabel went out to their car and brought in several large bags. "Oh!" said Alice you have so much stuff. It must have cost a fortune. You shouldn't have".

"Oh yes we should" said Harry. "I haven't seen Mabel so happy since our kids were small. She was like a kid the last week or so. This is the nicest Christmas I have had for years. Most of this stuff didn't cost anything. Some of it is second hand, but the kids won't know. It came from out of town" Ed was thinking of the fiasco with the used clothing not too long ago. He knew Alice did not want a repeat of that.

There were four of the most beautiful dolls Alice had ever seen. None of her children had ever had a real doll before. She had made every doll they ever had. "These are so beautiful" she began to cry. There was a ball for little Harry, and a big fire truck. "This is a truck that young Ted found in the trash. He found some of these other things too. I think someone cleaned out their kid's toy box before Christmas to make way for new. Ted took them home and did a little reconstruction and painting. They look enough like new, that the kids will never know". From another bag Mabel pulled the china set that she had spoke to Alice about. It was service for six. Tiny plates, cups and saucers and teapot.

"There is just one stipulation Ed said. We plan to spend the night right here. We don't want the children to know where this came from, but we want to see the looks on their little faces tomorrow morning. If it is better than the look on their mother's face right now, it will be priceless".

"You are certainly welcome to stay. You can sleep in our bed. I can sleep on the couch here and Harry will sleep on the sofa".

"Oh! No joked Ed. We take the couch and the sofa. You two will sleep in your own bed as usual. We want to see how Santa comes down that chimney".

By this time it was almost two thirty in the morning. Harry said "Well if the jolly old fellow is going to come down that chimney tonight, we had better go to bed. The kids will be bouncing down those stairs in about three hours whether we are ready or not".

They all went to bed and sure enough at about five thirty Alice heard conversation coming from the girl's room.

"Go back to sleep" Irene said to Jean. It is still dark. Santa probably didn't even come yet. If we go downstairs we might scare him away".

"But I'm not sleepy" said Jean "It must be morning".

"Well it isn't morning. We must wait until daylight. It takes Santa all night to deliver all the packages. We can't get up until daylight".

"Mommy" Jean called "Is it morning yet"?

"No" said Alice "go back to sleep. You will wake the others. It is not time to get up"

"But I am not sleepy" said Jean

"Close your eyes and pretend you are asleep. Be very quiet. If you are really quiet for a few minutes you will be able to go back to sleep".

"But I can't go back to sleep"

Alice decided there were three things she could do. She could allow Jean to wake the other children. That would mean that they would be very happy for an hour, and then be tired and irritable for the rest of the day. She could allow Jean to crawl into their bed. That would possibly start something that she did not want. Or she could get up, and go into their room to quiet the child. She decided on the latter. Getting up from her warm bed she dragged herself into the girl's room.

She crawled into the bed beside Jean, and put her arm around her. "Go back to sleep honey, it is a long time until morning". With her mother's arm around her, Jean fell back to sleep.

Morning did come eventually, and all of the children traipsed downstairs to find that Aunt Mabel and Uncle Ed were still there. As always Alice insisted that they have breakfast before going into the parlor to see what Santa had brought.

"Did it storm last night?" Irene asked Mabel. "Did you and Uncle Ed get snowed in?"

"No child, but we were just too tired to go home. It was really late, and Uncle Ed does not like to drive the snowy roads at night. We just spent the night. You don't mind do you?"

"Of course not" she replied.

They had breakfast of oatmeal and toast. The adults had coffee. Ed and Mabel were as anxious as the children for Harry to open the door to the parlor. When he did so, the children made a dash for the small Christmas tree, which they had lovingly helped their father to decorate the day before. There were so many presents they didn't know what to look at first. There were a lot of little things like they had never seen before. After they had hugged the dolls, and exclaimed over the dishes. There was a set of jacks some color books and crayons, some 'pick up sticks'. There were several books and a dictionary. There was a checkers game and Chinese checkers.

"Now you can learn to play together. These games are no fun to play alone. You will need to learn how to play together. Think how nice it would have been to have had all these things when Audrey was hurt. It would have been more fun for everyone, especially your mommy" said Aunt Mabel.

Alice could only marvel at the happiness in that room. And yesterday she had been so desperate because here was another Christmas with nothing for her children. "Thank God" she thought. "Thank God" and thank her dear friends and relatives.

Chapter 16

It was a terribly nasty storm. It hit one afternoon in mid March. It started to snow around three o'clock in the afternoon. When Harry came in from work he stopped at Mabel's. "It looks like this is going to be a bad one" he said. "I would like for you to keep the girls here tonight. I will bring them clean clothes in the morning. I don't think they should be walking home in this. I could wait for them and walk with them, but they would have to come back alone tomorrow so I think it would be best for them to stay here if you don't mind".

"Of course I don't mind" said Mabel. "It would be foolish for them to weather this storm if it is not necessary. Don't worry about them; I will keep them until the storm is over".

Harry went home that evening and told Alice that the girls would be staying at Mabel's. "I am so glad that Mabel likes our girls and is willing to take them so often. But I wish we did live closer to the school. It seems like we impose on her so much".

"She really doesn't mind" he said. "She likes an excuse to spoil them. And I do think they can stand a little spoiling. This last couple of years has been hard on them too. I am glad that they really don't understand a lot of this. But Irene is beginning to learn about the situation, and it hurts me to know that she will soon be feeling it worse".

"Well maybe when spring comes things will brighten up a little. I don't mind having to scrimp and save, I just don't want it to affect our girls"

Before they went to bed that night Harry filled the boiler with water
and put it on the stove. He always did this on the night before Alice
was to do laundry. When he awoke the next morning he started the
fire going in the stove. Alice fixed his breakfast and packed his lunch.
He left for work at around five fifteen. Alice went back to bed because
she did not have the girls to get ready for school and the little ones
usually slept until around eight o'clock.

When the little ones woke Alice changed the baby and was sitting
beside the pot bellied stove dressing Little Harry. The gown she had
on was flannel. The stove was very hot. Not realizing that she was so
close to the stove, Alice moved around on the chair in such a way that
the gown caught fire. Realizing that she was on fire, she dropped the
baby, and started to run. Since Alice always did the wrong thing in an
emergency, she started to run out doors. Fortunately, or unfortunately,
as she ran through the kitchen, she remembered the water on the
stove. "Water" she thought. "Put out the fire". She picked up the boiler
and poured it down over her back. Under normal circumstances, she
would not have had the strength to lift that heavy vat of water over her
head and pour that water over her body. But she seemed to have super
human strength. The water put the fire out, but unfortunately, it had
been near boiling. She scalded herself over the burns. She was
screaming with pain. Her children were screaming with fear. Little
Jean who was just five years old came running downstairs. When she
saw her mother she started to cry. Alice asked her to get a blanket.
Alice's clothes had been burned and they dropped to the floor. Alice
sat on a chair. She was naked, and charred black. Jean got the blanket,
and put it around her mother the best she could. She then got her coat
and her boots and put them on. She started out to find help. It was
nearly a mile to the closest neighbor. She trudged through the storm.
She had forgotten gloves, and hat. She was so cold that as she cried
the tears froze on her face. But she kept going. Finally she came to
a house. She tried to knock on the door, but her hands were so cold
it hurt to knock. She leaned against the door and screamed.

NYDA A. WRIGHTSMAN

Mrs. Friend heard what she thought was her cat. She never let the cat in the house, but it was such a cold day she felt sorry for the poor cat being left out doors. She finally decided she would just bring her in and get her warmed up. When she opened her door a child literally fell in the door. The child said "call my Aunt Mabel, My mommy's burned bad."

Mrs. Friend knew that there was something serious wrong at the Jackson home. Alice would never have let this child out on a day like this if there was not something terrible wrong. She immediately called Mabel and told her. "One of the Jackson kids just fell in my door. She says her mother is burned bad. It must be bad. The child is nearly frozen" she said. "I will care for her but you must get someone out to the house to see what is wrong."

It so happened that the weather was so bad that morning that the men could not work. Harry had started home and stopped to tell Mabel that the children needed to stay another night. When Mabel hung up the phone she said "You must get home as fast as you can. Something is terribly wrong at your house. Just go". As she finished telling him to go, she grabbed the phone and called her husband. Then she grabbed her coat. Harry ran as fast as he could for home. When he reached the house he could smell burned meat. When he opened the door, he nearly fainted from shock. His wife was sitting on a chair in the kitchen. She was burned black. The blanket that Jean had wrapped around her shoulders had fallen to the floor. Her cries were merely moans.

He took one look and knew that there was absolutely nothing he could do for her. He had never felt so helpless in his life. He studied the situation for a minute, and then turned to run back to get Mabel. She was coming on the porch. She had run all the way too.

When Mabel sized up the situation she said "I called Ed before I left the house, He is on his way. Go back to town and bring my car out here. I don't think you can take the road, but you have to find a way. We have to get her back to my house. Ed will be able to take care of

118

her better there. Harry turned and ran all the way back to town.

Mabel looked for something that might take the sting out of the burn. She saw nothing but a gallon of apple butter. "At this stage it couldn't hurt" she thought. "I must make her think I can do something. She is going into shock. I must calm her". She smeared that apple butter on some of the burns. It seemed to help a little. She knew it was not doing anything but she was trying to keep Alice from going into shock. "If she would pass out it would be better" she thought. "Being conscious she is feeling all this pain". To Alice she said "It will be okay Alice. Harry has gone for my car. We will get you to my house. Ed is on the way. We will take care of you. Try to stay calm".

Mabel calmed the babies down some. There was no way she could keep them from seeing their mother in such agony. She tried to assure them that their Mommy would be okay. But in her heart she knew she was lying to them. "I don't see how she can live through this" she thought. "Oh! God help my brother and his children." she prayed.

It took Harry almost two hours to drive the two miles to the house. He cut one farmer's fence in three places, and drove across the cemetery. He tried to stay near the fence so that he wouldn't drive on any graves, but he was not sure if he did.

Finally he got to the house where he had left Alice and Mabel. He thanked God that his wife was still alive. When they tried to get Alice off the chair she screamed. She stuck fast to the chair and some of the flesh fell off her bones. "Get a clean sheet" said Mabel "We need that next to her flesh. We can't use a blanket. It will stick to her flesh too". Alice screamed every time they touched her. She was in so much pain they could not even touch her, Blisters hung from her arms like butterfly wings. The only thing they could do was to wrap her in that sheet, and put her in the car. Mabel sat in the back seat and held her, and they both cried. Harry was also crying. They prayed that somehow this would turn out alright. But none held much hope. Alice was burned on almost half of her body. Most of it was third degree burns. It looked so hopeless, but they could not give up.

When they reached Mabel's house, they again had to just pick her up and carry her inside. Alice's screams were now just low moans. Alice was praying to die. They were praying for her to live.

They decided it would be better for her to be downstairs. Mabel told Harry "Go upstairs and take apart the bed in the first room on the right. Bring it down. We will set it up in the library. I'm sure Ed will want to take her to the hospital, but for now this will have to do" The closest hospital was nearly fifty miles away.

Chapter 17

While Harry was taking apart the bed, Mabel was moving the furniture from the library. She put the couch in the parlor, and a couple of chairs in the dining room. When Harry brought down the bed, they put it up in the library. Mabel got fresh sheets, and blankets. They managed to get Alice onto the bed on her stomach.

It was about that time that the girls came from school for lunch. Mabel said to Irene, "Go to the kitchen and make some peanut butter sandwiches. Help with the little ones while we take care of your mother."

"What happened? Oh! Daddy what happened to Mama?"

"She was burned really badly. Please just do as you are told. We need you to be big girls now and help take care of the little ones. I think you can stay home this afternoon. You can be of some help, and I know you will not be able to concentrate on school until we stabilize your Mother. Now please go make some sandwiches like aunt Mabel told you."

"Okay Daddy."

Mrs. Friend gathered Jean up in her arms and carried her to the couch. The child was so cold it scared her. "Let's get you warmed up some" She said. "First let's get these cold wet clothes off. She removed Jeans clothing. Even her underwear was wet and frozen to her body. When she took off the boots, she realized that this child had to have dressed herself, and in quite a hurry. She had no socks, and no shoes under those boots. She had no hat and no mittens.

Mrs. Friend wrapped her in a warm blanket and held her in her arms. The child kept shivering, and crying muffled little sounds. "You poor child" she said. "You are nearly frozen. I don't know how long you were out there in that blizzard, but you are lucky to even be alive. Let's just sit here for awhile and get warm. Your clothes will dry in a little while. I can probably find something to dress you in, but for now we will just stay wrapped in this blanket".

She carried her to the rocking chair and sat down and started to rock. As Jean began to get warm and quit shivering she started to fall asleep. Mrs. Friend did not know if this was a good thing. She had heard that sometimes after trauma you should keep the victim awake so that you could observe her. Was that only for head trauma? Maybe to be safe she should keep the child awake. So she gently woke the child, and started to ask questions.

"Do you feel better now? Are you getting warm?"

The child shook her head but did not say a word. "Can you speak to me? You are Jean aren't you?"

Again the child just shook her head. She was still sobbing little moans. For some time all she seemed to be able to do was to whine and shake her head. Mrs. Friend kept her awake by asking questions but the child just made small murmuring sounds. The older lady did not have any idea what to do with this poor child. She knew that it was no use to call Mabel again. Whatever had happened out at the Jackson house, she was sure must be something bad. She could not get the child to talk and she didn't want to alarm her more. So she just kept talking to her.

Finally after what seemed like hours, but was probably about half an hour, the child started to talk. All at once she let out a burst of words. 'My mommy was on fire, she was on fire. Oh we were all so scared. She was hurt bad. Mama dropped Harry on the floor. Mama needs my daddy. Did you call my Aunt Mabel? Please call my Aunt Mabel. She needs to find my Daddy. Somebody needs to find my Daddy. Oh!

Please please help me find my daddy." The child was crying and shaking so hard she was almost uncontrollable.

"I called your aunt Mabel dear. I am sure she has found your Daddy. They will help your Mommy". When the older woman heard the child say "Mommy was on fire" she was frantic. Was the house on fire? There were two babies in that house. What about the other children? Was Mabel able to find help? She had to learn something. She decided to take a chance on calling Mabel again. Maybe someone was there. She dialed the number, and waited. There was no answer. She waited for about twenty minutes and tried again. There was still no answer. She went to the window and looked out toward the Jackson home. She did not see any smoke. If the house was on fire wouldn't there be smoke? Hopefully the house was not on fire. She would just have to sit and wait. When her phone rang, she nearly jumped out of her shoes. It was Mabel. "I don't have much time" she said "But I need to know. How is Jean? I don't know how that child managed to get as far as your house in this weather. We are so worried about her".

"I think Jean will be okay" said Mrs. Friend. "She was nearly frozen to death. It took a long while to get her warmed up. She had on her coat over her gown, and her boots with no shoes or socks. But I think she will be ok. I don't know how she made it this far without freezing to death. Do you know what happened out there? Jean told me that her mother was on fire."

"Yes. It is really bad."

"Was the house on fire?"

"No, it is a long story, and we have just brought her to my house. She is .in really bad shape. I don't have time for details, but if you can handle Jean for a couple of hours, we will appreciate it. We just had to know that she is ok"

"Don't worry about her. I think she will be alright. I have her clothes drying by the fireplace. They will be dry soon and I will put them back on her. Please keep me informed."

"We will. Thank you." And Mabel hung up the phone.

The child kept asking about her mother. She seemed to be so worried. Mrs. Friend couldn't help but wonder what this child had seen this morning. She tried all afternoon to keep her mind on other things, but every little while she would start again asking if her Mommy was going to be alright. Mrs. Friend tried to reassure her, but she knew that in her voice the child was hearing "I'm lying to you child. Your mother is dying"

After a few hours by the fire, the clothes were dry, and warm. She helped Jean to put them back on. She found a pair of socks to put on her feet. "We will need to have someone bring you some clothes if you are going to stay here for a little while. You need your shoes. We will see about that later. Let's see if we can find you some lunch. Are you hungry? How would you like some milk and cookies?"

Jean just smiled and shook her head. While Mrs. Friend was getting ready to give Jean milk and cookies, she realized that the child had probably not even had breakfast. If she had, she was sure she would have been dressed and had on some shoes and socks under those boots. So rather than cookies she opted for a bowl of hot soup and some toast. The child ate like she was famished. "Now how about that milk and cookies."

Jean smiled at her and said "Yes please."

After her lunch she thought that if she could get her to take a nap, she would get her mind off of her mother. She tried to rock her, but the child would have none of that. Helen thought that this child, the middle child of the family, probably had not been rocked to sleep since infancy. She didn't seem to be sleepy anyway. She found some paper and a couple of crayons in a junk drawer which had not been cleaned out for years. She tried to help Jean to draw. She was surprised to see that this five year old could draw pretty well. She seemed to really enjoy drawing, so Helen just kept encouraging her to draw more pictures.

When James Friend came home he was surprised and pleased to

see that his wife had a little visitor. He was rather pleased to see her having such a good time with this child. Their children were all grown and had children of their own, but had moved away years ago. They only saw their grandchildren about once a year, and then only for a day or two. They missed having children around. Mr. Friend took Jean up on his lap and they played nursery rhyme games. Soon he had her laughing and singing. He got down on the floor with her and played like a kid. She rode on his back. "My Daddy plays this game with us sometimes. I like this game" she said. They played until James was about worn out. He got up and sat in his chair. He said to his wife, "Boy I guess I am really getting old. This little child has worn me out. But I have really had fun."

Then to Jean he said, "Are you tired too."

"No let's do it some more."

"I'm sorry sweetie but I need a little rest first."

But he was a little disappointed when Harry came to pick up the child that evening.

Ed was visibly shocked when he saw Alice. Oh! My God! I think she should be in the hospital. Let's get her stabilized and then I will call to see if they can take her. I don't know if I can take care of this here. He worked on Alice more than an hour. Every time he touched her she screamed. He had never seen anything worse than this. He didn't tell anyone, not even his wife, but he was sure Alice would die. This was the worst burn he had ever seen. She needed to be in a hospital.

When he had put ointment all over the burns, and given Alice a shot for the pain, he went to the phone and called the closest hospital. After explaining the circumstances, and giving them the information on the condition of the patient, he was told that if Harry did not have insurance, they would need a hefty deposit or they would not take her.

Of course Harry had no insurance. Ed called every government agency he knew of but could not find any help. Harry was not eligible for any government assistance.

Chapter 18

Ed sat Harry down and had a talk with him. He explained that this was the worst burn he had ever seen. "It is a wonder she is still alive, Harry. I have to be honest with you. We have a real fight on our hands. Even in the hospital I would only give her a thirty percent chance. She is critical. I will do my best, Harry but I am afraid we might lose her. You need to know that. There is so much danger of infection and dehydration. Even in the hospital she would be in danger of infection. Burns that deep are bound to become infected some. We will be fighting an uphill battle all the way. To be honest with you though, I feel that she might be better off here. I really don't like some of the way they treat these really bad burns. Removing the dead skin the way they do, is terribly painful for the patient. I would like to try something else. You know Mabel will take the very best care of her. If those burns were in the front, she wouldn't have a chance. By them being on her back, I don't think they have reached any vital organs. I do worry about her lungs. It is hard to know how much smoke she may have inhaled. If she inhaled or swallowed smoke, her lungs will have been weakened. There is danger of Pneumonia. These things we won't know for awhile."

Harry could not hold back the tears. He wept like a child. "Ed" said Harry "I can see that she is critical. I don't know what I would do without her. She is my whole life. I need her, and the kids need her. If I can't get her into the hospital, then there is only one choice. I hate to even have to ask you and Mabel to do this, but I have no other choice, and I know that both of you will do your best. I feel like you have already done so much for us. I have faith in you. If anyone can save her Ed, I know it is you. Just tell me what I can do to help"

"First of all, I would suggest you ask members of your family to take the children. Mabel will have her hands full. We need to find temporary homes for your kids. Mabel loves the kids, but she would not be able to take even one of the kids and still take care of Alice, This will be a full time job for months. If we can save her, it will take from six months to a year. You must know that".

"I will find places for the kids. Thank God we both have big loving families. I am sure that Alice's brothers will help. I will have to talk to the kids tonight. Irene, Audrey and Jean are the ones who will put up a fight I am sure. But I will handle that. I don't think the two little ones will really care who takes care of them as long as somebody loves them. I have to go to Mrs. Friend's this evening and get Jean. She was certainly a brave little girl to have done what she did. I want her to know that we love her even more for it. She has been with a stranger all day, and I don't want her to think I have deserted her".

"I am going to keep Alice sedated for at least a few days Ed said. "As long as she is awake, she will be in terrible pain. It won't subside any time soon".

"I will leave her in your capable hands Ed. Can I talk to her now, or is she out of it"?

"I think she is coherent right now. I have given her a shot and it is starting to take affect".

Harry went to the side of the bed and said "Alice, can you hear me?"

"Um hum" she moaned.

"I am going to go get Jean, and I have some things I have to do. Ed and Mabel will take care of you. Honey I don't want to leave you right now, but I must. I love you"

"Um hum?"

With that Harry left the room leaving his wife in the capable hands of his brother-in-law.

When Harry knocked on Mrs. Friend's door she knew it was him. She had seen him come around the house and up the steps. She opened the door, and Jean came running. "Daddy" she said. "Daddy" She jumped into his arms and put her little arms around his neck. "Daddy, Mommy is hurt real bad"

"Yes sweetheart, Mommy is hurt real bad. She is at Aunt Mabel's house now. You are a brave little girl for finding help for your Mommy".

"Daddy is Mommy going to die?"

"We hope not darling. Uncle Ed and Aunt Mabel are going to try to make her better"

"Just what did happen out there this morning?" asked Mrs. Friend.

"She was dressing Harry by the stove, and her gown caught fire. As near as we can tell, she picked up the boiler of water from the stove, and poured it over herself to put out the fire not realizing that the water was scalding hot. She scalded herself over the burns. It is bad, really bad".

"Mabel has taken her to their house. Ed came in a few hours ago. He says it will take a miracle. But I am expecting one. They won't take Alice in the hospital because I have no insurance. Ed and Mabel are going to try to save her right here. I believe maybe they can. That's why I said I am expecting a miracle. I have to find temporary homes for my kids for awhile. Mabel will be taking care of Alice, so I have to find a place for my kids to go. It is good that we have large loving families. Mom and Dad will take Irene. Alice's brother John has said he will take the two little ones. I am going to see if my sister Agnes won't keep Audrey. That way the girls won't have to change schools".

"Well if you would let me, I would be glad to keep this little one for as long as you need me to. She has been a blessing to me today. We have had a wonderful time. She was awfully worried about her mother, but we got along fine. And James has been having the time of his life since he came home this evening. James called from his chair "She didn't even cry when I sang 'Froggie Went A Courtin'

Harry laughed. "She doesn't cry when I sing to her either. She is a brave little girl"

Would you like to stay here with me while your mommy gets better?" Helen said.

"I want my mommy" said Jean.

"Sure you do" said Mrs. Friend. "Just so you know Harry, I would be glad to keep this one or one of the others if you would like. Just let me know. I don't think I could handle the littlest one; I am a little too old for middle of the night feedings and such. But I am willing to keep one of them for you. Just say the word".

"I will keep that in mind" said Harry. "Right now I will take her to see her mommy and we will get back to you. Thank you for everything you did today".

You are welcome, and if there is anything at all I can do, let me know. We are here if you need us.

"Thank you again" said Harry. He took his little girl by the hand and went back down the street.

Melva Pearl was a middle aged woman with long salt and pepper hair which she wore in a bun on top of her head. Her husband Robert was editor of the weekly newspaper. He left the house each morning around seven thirty, and usually did not return until late evening.

Over the last few years her marriage had seemed to wither away. Not that she didn't love Robert, she did. And she did not believe that he had stopped loving her, but somehow they seemed to be in a rut. They had tried for fifteen years to have a baby, but it was not to be. She had three miscarriages, and the doctor said they should give it up. At first they had wanted to adopt, but after a few years they had given up on that too.

Melva had several nieces and nephews which she spoiled rotten. She loved children, but had realized years ago that she would never be a mother. When she heard about these children who might need temporary homes for a few months, she jumped at the chance to help. One of these little girls would be a lot of company for her. She knew the Jackson woman. That lady had made her a dress once. It was one of the nicest dresses she owned. Harry was that young man who was always so nice to everyone. He would help anyone do anything. Someone needed to help him now.

When Robert came home that evening, Melba asked him "What would you think if I volunteered to take one of those Jackson kids for awhile. It looks like their mother might die. I guess she is in terrible shape. She was nearly killed this morning. Somehow she caught on fire and ran. Helen Friend told me that one of those little kids ran to her for help. I guess the poor child was nearly frozen when she got to Helen's place".

"Do you really want to take in a child who might lose her mother? Do you realize what a traumatic thing that would be? It would be heartbreaking for both of you. I know how soft hearted you are. If this woman dies, what will happen to all those kids?"

"I don't know dear, but I know that sometimes I get so lonely here with you gone so much. Maybe it is selfish, but I think I could help one of those kids and I know that she would be so much company for me Do you think I should call Mabel and ask if I can help?"

"If you want to do this I have no objections. As long as you do understand what you may be letting yourself in for. If you become attached to this child and then they take her from you, can you handle that?"

"Robert, I know she will not ever be mine. Whether her mother lives of dies, she will not be mine".

"I am going to call first thing in the morning."

Next morning Melba awoke early. She could almost feel one of those little girls in her arms. She waited until nearly nine o'clock before she went to the phone to call Mabel. When Mabel answered the phone she started right in. "Mabel, I heard about your sister-in-law's accident. How is she"?

Well it doesn't look good. She is holding her own, but it is really a bad situation Melva. It has been touch and go all night. We were up most of the night with her. It is the worst I ever saw. Ed says it will take a miracle. We are really worried".

Well. I heard that Harry is looking for temporary places to put his kids for awhile. I just wanted to let you know that I would love to take one of them. I can only imagine what those poor kids must be going through, and I would like to be able to help if possible. Tell Harry to just keep me in mind when he is deciding what to do".

"I will tell him that. I know he is hoping to keep the two older girls in town because he does not want to have to uproot them and make them change schools on top of this. Mom wants Irene to stay there with her and Dad I don't think he has a plan for Audrey yet".

"I hope he will consider letting me take one of them. It would be nice for me to have someone other than myself to think of for awhile.

When Harry came in that afternoon, Mabel told him about Melva's phone call. "That's great" said Harry. "John will take the little ones. I will ask Helen Friend to take Jean. She wants to take care of her, and if Melva takes Audrey that will be great. Irene is with Mom and Dad. The older three will be here in town, so they will not get quite so homesick.

Harry managed to get his children temporary homes. Each child was in a different place. But each child was in a home where he or she was loved and cared for. The three older girls were staying with people in town. This meant that Irene and Audrey would not have to change schools and they were also where they could see their mother often. Alice wished that her children didn't have to see her like that, and she was glad that the little ones were not able to see her this way. Irene was with Harry's mother and Dad. Audrey was with Mrs. Pearl and Jean was with Mrs. Friend. Alice's brother John said that he thought that the two babies should be kept together. "They are so young. They can't understand any of this. But if they are together they will have some feeling of family. They won't see the others often, but they will know they are brother and sister".

That evening Harry took the two girls up the street to their new temporary homes. "Now" he said, I know you girls will miss your mother. You may not go to Aunt Mabel's unless Uncle Ed says you can. You are big enough to understand that your Mama is really hurt bad. Uncle Ed is trying to make her better, and Aunt Mabel has all she can do to take care of her".

"We know Daddy" said Audrey. She was crying short little sobs. "I will try not to cry all the time. I promise I will try to be a good girl. I will miss you too Daddy".

"Me too" cried Jean. "I will be a good girl. Mrs. Friend is a nice lady and I like her. And Mr. Friend took me for a piggy back ride like you do sometimes" she laughed and said "He said I wored him out".

"I know this is hard for all of you, but right now we have to think about your Mama. Everything we do for awhile will have to be to help Mama. Uncle Ed will let you see her sometimes. But he is worried about infection. Sometimes we carry little tiny germs on our clothes, and we don't even know it. If Mama gets some of them on her, it will be very bad. It is hard for little girls to understand. Aunt Mabel thinks I tell you girls too much. She thinks you should not know just how bad things really are. I believe that you can help Mama more if you know what is going on. That is why I try to let you know everything I think you need to know".

When they reached Mrs. Friend's door, Jean knocked on the door. When Mrs. Friend came to the door she picked Jean up and hugged her. "Hello Sweetheart" she said. "Come on in. I hope you will like staying with me".

"I'm sure I will like it here ok. I promised Daddy that I will not cry too much".

"When you feel like crying, you let me know, I will give you a hug. Maybe that will help.

"Okay" said Jean. Then she said "You can go now, Daddy. I will be ok"

Harry and Audrey went on up the street. Just as they reached the Pearl house Robert Pearl pulled into the drive. They walked onto the porch together. Robert opened the door and called, "Melva, We have company". Melva came from the kitchen with a smile on her face. "What are you doing home so early?" she asked. "I wanted to help you greet our new little guest, and I got here just in time" he said. Harry said to Audrey "You do know these people don't you Audrey?"

"Yes" she said. Mr. Pearl works in the newspaper office. Our school class visited there once. And I came here a couple of times to play with Jimmy".

"Jimmy?" asked Harry.

"Jimmy is my nephew" said Melva. 'He visits often and the children often play together".

"Oh! I see" said Harry. "I brought some clothes for her. She goes to school so you will get a break from her for the day. You and she can decide if she is to take her lunch or come home at lunch time. I don't think you will have any problems with her, she has promised to try to be good. If you have any problems let me know".

"We won't have any problems, will we Audrey?"

"No, Mrs. Pearl. I will try to be good."

Chapter 19

Harry went back to the house to do his chores each day after work. There was still work to be done, and he needed the money he was making there. He was also working on the road thirty hours a week. Harry tried to at least pay for the ointments and medicine which Ed was using for Alice. It was hard to believe how much they cost. Ed bought the ointment by the gallon. He used half a gallon of ointment each day in the beginning. It was about ten days into the treatment several spots on Alice's back became infected. One was the spot where the meat had fallen off onto the chair when they picked her up to put her in the car that first day. She had swollen to almost twice her size, and green fluid was coming from a lot of the blisters. Ed told Mabel to boil some water and to let it cool to lukewarm. He wanted sterile water. They waited until the water was cool enough to put onto Alice's skin. Then they cleansed the burns with the sterile water. Alice screamed at first, but as they were able to clean the area, it began to feel better. Each day they used this treatment on different areas of Alice's back and arms.

It seemed that when they managed to clear up one infection, another place managed to start seeping the green poison. They were constantly fighting infection. Alice was getting weaker by the day. Every time they saw a little improvement in one spot, there was a problem in another. Mabel would cleanse the wounds for awhile, and when Alice seemed as though she could not stand any more, Mabel would let it rest for half an hour and try again. It was a long drawn out process. Even tough it was terribly painful, it had to be done. Mabel felt like she was torturing Alice, but she had seen what that green poison could do. She knew that her friend was slowly dying, and she had to stop this poison now. She cried with Alice as they worked to clean the infection from her arms and back. It was still almost impossible to move Alice at all, and when they did it was torture for all of them. They could not let the children even be in the house while they were treating her. It was too much torture for the adults. They could not let the children even near their mother when she was being treated.

Mabel watched as her friend became more and more lethargic. It seemed that Alice had simply lost the will to live. Alice lay on her stomach without being able to move a muscle. The dressings needed to be changed twice a day, and the areas cleansed once each day. Feeding her was a real task. She could barely raise her head, and in order for Mabel to feed her she would need to put towels under Alice's head, and try to spoon feed her without missing her mouth. Harry would stop each evening on his way home from work. It broke his heart to see his wife in so much pain .Ed came home twice a week just to check on her progress. Several times Mabel called him to come home because she thought it was the end. His job as a company doctor in a mining town kept him away several days at a time. It was six weeks before they were able to even turn Alice to her side for a few minutes at a time. After about eight weeks they were able to get her up into a chair. Sitting was a problem, so she could only sit for a few minutes each time, but they got her up at least twice a day. Gradually Alice began to want to live again. She told Mabel that when they were all praying for her to live, she had been praying to die. Then when it really hit her that they had to send all her children away, she realized that it was selfish for her to want to die. She decided she had to live so that she could get her family back together.

For a couple of weeks Ed had insisted that the children not be allowed to see Alice. He was afraid that they may carry in something to cause infection, and there was already too much infection and Alice was showing signs of becoming dehydrated, which would lead to worse infection. As the danger of infection became less likely, he did allow the girls to come into the room, but they were not allowed to touch their mother. They were to stand three feet from her. The girls did not like the rules, but Ed had explained that if their mother got more infection she could still die or at best get worse again. They did not want to do anything to make her worse, so they obeyed the rules to the letter.

In spite of all the turmoil in the family, the girls were doing very well in school. It seemed that since their mother had been injured, most of the children had quit teasing them. Mabel thought "Thank heavens for small miracles". Even Audrey's glasses seemed to have been accepted by the other children. Or maybe Harry had scared all of them when he caught the Smith boys at the cemetery. Maybe it was respect, or fear of Harry that caused this change. "Whatever it is" thought Mabel "we will accept it".

Finally one day in mid May Ed told Harry that if he wanted to have the children all to come to see their mother, they could visit her on the coming week end. Ed went to Alice's brother's house to pick up the babies and bring them to see Alice. It was time to put some life back into the family. He thought that if she could see all of the children for a little while, it would give her a reason to work harder. Rehabilitation would be a long drawn out process, and she needed a little incentive.

Ed told Alice "We are going to have all the children here. We want them to see that you are finally going to be alright. You need to see them too. And they need to see each other too. The babies have not seen any of the family for two months. But you must promise that if it becomes too much, you will tell me. I know you want to see all of them. But this will be harder than you think. You are still very weak, and the babies are stronger than you think. We will only let them visit for a little while then they must go again. You realize that you cannot handle it for long. It might be better to have one at a time, but I think you need to see them all at once".

"Yes, I do need to see all of them at once. Even for five minutes. Sometimes it seems that I have been in a terrible nightmare, and that none of it is real. Please Ed let them all come in for a few minutes. Then they can go again. I will feel so much better if I can see all of them at once. I will know that things are going to be ok".

"You need to know" said Ed "that you are not completely out of the woods. You have several places that have not closed completely. There is still some danger, but I think I can safely say we are over the worst of it. I am very pleased with your progress. But now comes the hard part. Every muscle in your body has weakened. You will need to start strengthening them now. Your job these next few months will be to become strong enough to start taking care of these babies yourself again. It will be hard work but you can do it".

"How much longer do you think it will be Ed"?

"That depends largely on you Alice. You can only stand so much pain, and there will still be a lot. You just need to do your best, and let God take care of the rest. We can only do so much at a time and there is a lot we must do yet.

"This will be the hardest job you ever did, but the most rewarding".

"I know that, and I am ready. Or at least I will be, after I see my kids."

"Today is the happiest day of my life" Alice said to Harry. "I am going to see all of my children together again... You don't think Mary will forget me do you. How long has it been?"

"It has only been a little more than two months. But honey, she was only a couple of months old when this happened. She hardly had time to know you. But don't borrow trouble. If she doesn't remember you, I promise it won't be long before she does. It won't be as long before you see them next time. Soon we will be at home and all of us will be together again".

About that time the door opened, and in came five very happy children. Irene was carrying Mary. As soon as the baby saw Alice she stretched out her little arms.

"Oh! She likes me anyway" said Alice. "Come here sweetheart"

"Mary likes everyone Mama. She is really a friendly little thing" said Irene. I wish we could see her every day and play with her".

"Mama" said little Harry. This was the first time the two smaller ones had seen their mother since the day after the accident. Alice was crying great tears of joy.

"I love you Mommy" said Irene. And that was echoed by each of the other girls"

"I love all of you so much" said Alice. "I hate not being able to be with you".

"We don't like it either Mama but we just want you to get better"

"I am working very hard at that. But tell me. How are you doing? Do you like Mrs. Pearl, Audrey?

"I really like Mr. and Mrs. Pearl. They are really nice Mama. But I hope you get well soon so that you can come home".

"I do too dear".

"Mama" said Jean. "Mr. Friend made me a cradle for my dolly. He even let me help him hammer nails. It was fun".

"Maybe we will have a new little carpenter in the family".

"Mr. Pearl takes us to get ice cream every Sunday evening. He said that is not spoiling me, it is just loving me. Do you think he is spoiling me, mama? Mrs. Pearl said she don't think you would like for him to spoil me".

"Maybe it is ok to spoil you just a bit" said Alice as she reached out to hug her child.

Harry was helping Alice to hold the two babies on her lap. He could see that Alice was uncomfortable

"Okay kids" he said. "Mommy can't sit this way for long. Why don't you sit on Daddy's lap, and hold Mommy's right hand for a little while. It is uncomfortable for Mama to hold you. Remember, Mama still needs to get much better before she can take care of all of us".

"Mama" said Irene" School will be out next week. I think I will get some A's on my report card. Grandpa said he thinks I should get an A in arithmetic. He helps me with my homework. He makes numbers seem like fun".

"That's great" said her mother. "I know you can do well when you try.

Each of the older girls hugged Alice very carefully as if they were afraid she would break. Alice's arms and back were still covered with bandages. Ed stood watching the little family reunion. He couldn't help but think how this could have turned out so much differently. He was so glad to see this day come. He thanked God for helping him to help this little family. He knew that without God's help this reunion would not have been possible. He also knew that they were still on an up hill climb, but he thought "Now I think I can see the light at the end of the tunnel. This is what I went to school all those years for". He couldn't stop the feeling of pride swelling up in him.

"Ten more minutes" he said. "Then this reunion will be over for today". Then looking at Harry he said "I will take Harry and Mary back to John's after supper. They can spend a few hours with you and the girls. But I think Alice has had about enough for today" He then left the room leaving the little family to say goodbye to their mother.

It was a tearful goodbye. The babies were not old enough to understand but the older children helped Harry to pry them away from the room. It broke Alice's heart to know that it would probably be weeks again before she saw her babies. Even knowing that, she was happy to have seen them today. They would remember her, and still love her. That was enough for now.

Harry took the kids out into the yard that afternoon and played with them. They played hide and seek for awhile. They climbed the old apple tree. They ran around just having fun. It was a very happy day. Even though they all knew that at the end of the day, they would all go their separate ways again, they did not let that ruin their fun. They spent several hours just enjoying each other. When Mabel called them in for supper everything became quiet. They all stopped what they were doing, and stood looking at each other. They knew that this happy day was near an end. They all soberly walked inside. There was no crying, just sadness.

Chapter 20

As they ate supper in almost total silence Harry said "Kids, I promise you that soon we will all be together again. Your Mom needs a little more time to recuperate. She is working very hard and we all have to do the same. You have been great kids through all of this. We love all of you".

"We love you too Daddy" said all of the children at once. "And we love Mama too" said Jean.

"Daddy" said Irene. "Do you think we will move back to the big house when Mama gets better?"

"I don't think so dear" said Harry. "Mr. Kinney is trying to find someone to take my place. With my other job and with Mama being like she is, there is no way we can continue to do that work too. Mama was a big part of this job. Now she will need a lot of help herself, she won't be able to do much for a long time. I have asked Mr. Kinney to replace me"

"I will miss living in that house" said Audrey. "But I just want Mama to get better and come to live with us. Where will we live?"

"I am not quite sure yet honey". I am looking at a couple of houses but I am also looking for a better job. Things are looking better and maybe I will find a better job. If I do we may need to move away from here".

Mabel said "Harry, are you sure you want to be discussing this with your children"?

"I think my kids have been through things that no child should ever have to go through. I don't think they need to have any more surprises. If I do decide I want to do this, it will have to be a family decision". Alice agrees with me, that if we want the children to understand, they must know the circumstances of our decision.

"I hope you know what you are doing" said Mabel.

To the children he said "Your Uncle Paul went to Pennsylvania and got a job in the coal mines He says they are hiring a lot of men. We have been talking about what it might mean for us. We have to give up the job at the house because we can no longer keep up with it. This coal mining job sounds like a good opportunity for us. Remember we have not decided yet. We may not even do this at all. But I do need a decent job. If we decide to do this it will affect you children too. So we want you not to be shocked if we decide to move".

"I don't want to move" said Jean. "I like to live in the big house".

"That is no longer an option" said Harry. "That has already been decided I don't want any of you to worry right now. For now things have to stay as they are. I will not leave as long as your mother is not able to go too, so for now things stay the same. We will discuss this more later".

"How about some pie and ice cream now" asked Mabel?

After dinner was over, Ed took the babies back to Alice's brother John. John asked "how did it go?"

"It went very well" said Ed "Your sister has a lot of spunk. I know she was crying inside when she had to say goodbye again, but she did not show even one tear".

"Doc" said John "how long do you think it will be before she is able to at least walk?"

"She asked me almost the same question today. I will tell you exactly what I told her. That depends on her. She can only stand a certain amount of pain. There will be a lot more. We have to take it one day at a time. It will still be a few months at the least. She has made remarkable improvement. To be honest, I didn't expect her to live. I had never seen anyone with burns that bad. If I were a betting man, I would have lost my money. Of course I could have never told her family that, but I did tell Harry that first day when I saw her, I felt he had to prepare himself for the worst. I am so glad I was wrong".

"So am I Doc, so am I".

On the fourth of July, Alice's brother John brought the babies to see their mother again. He went in to her room alone first. He just felt that he needed to talk to her alone for a minute.

"John, I am so glad you are here" she said. "I need someone I can talk to. I know I can talk to you. Mabel is so good to me, but she can be a real tough task master. I know she is only helping me, but sometimes I just want to scream `leave me alone, give it a rest'. I am really trying to build up my strength, but it is so hard. I would have never thought it would be so hard to just learn to move again. It seems that the skin that I have growing back is not big enough for me. It is so tender. When I move it feels like I am stretching my skin too far, and that it might break. Oh John, it hurts so bad even to try to make a fist. The skin on my wrists feels so tight. The back of my knees, my neck, my elbows every joint I have feels like it can't stretch the skin far enough to move my joints. Mabel has me moving everything several times a day, but it seems that it is not improving at all. I thought that by now it would be healed more. I can't complain to Harry. He has so much on his mind. I just need a shoulder to cry on. Can I use yours?"

"You sure can, sis" he said. "It will always be there for you if you need it. You know that. You have been through Hell and back kiddo".

"It's been a long time since you called me that."

Alice wrapped her bandaged arms around her brother and cried like a baby.

"Oh John, I don't think I will ever get back to normal. Mabel and Ed say I am making so much progress, but it seems like I am in a rut, and I can't get out. I'm sorry" she said. "I feel so terrible. I know everybody I love has been suffering with me. But there are times when I just feel sorry for myself. I can't help it John, I do".

"You have a right to get depressed now and then. Anyone who has been through what you have been through would feel the same. I don't know how you made it Sis, but I am so glad you did. Now that things are looking up, and you are beginning to see the light at the end of the tunnel your nerves are a tangled mess. You have a right to feel however you want to feel".

"You know Harry's Brother Paul has gone to Pennsylvania and got a job in the coal mines. Harry thinks he should do the same. There is no work around here, and it doesn't look like there will be any for some time. I hate to see Harry go to the mines. That is such dangerous work, but we have been struggling for three years with no relief in sight. We have to so something.

"I know sis. It seems like Harry has been really down on his luck; I don't know the answer kiddo. But I do know that something has to give soon".

"Ok" she said pulling herself together and pulling away from him. "That is enough tears today. My babies are here and I want to see them". John handed her a tissue went out to get little Harry and Mary.

"Oh!" said Alice, "look how much you are growing, and I am missing so much of your life"

"Mama" they both said. Alice wrapped her arms around her babies and cried again. "Don't cry Mama" said little Harry.

"I am crying because I am so happy to see you" she said. "I love you so much"

"I love you this much" said Little Harry holding his arms out as far as he could. "I know darling" his mother told him.

John lifted the children up on the bed with their mother. She played with Mary's little toes. She held her little hands. She hugged little Harry so tight that it hurt her arms. How could she love them any more? She cried a little and then laughed a little.

After just a short time John could see that this was wearing on Alice. He said "Okay Kiddo, we need to finish this up. Now that you are on the mend, we can bring them a little more often. The reason that we didn't bring them more often was because Ed said we needed to try to prevent infection. You were not doing so well there for awhile, and Ed was afraid of infection. But he still says that we can't let you wear yourself out. We all know what you have been through, and we don't want to tire you. He said that I can bring them more often, and I will sis, I promise. I know you wish you could keep these little ones right there in that bed with you, but we all know that would not be good either."

"Ok kids, say bye-bye to Mama". The children whined a little, but let John remove them from the bed and they went out of the room

On his way out of the room John met Audrey and Melva. "Uncle John" said Audrey. "You came to see Mama."

To Melva she said "Mrs. Pearl, this is my Uncle John, and my baby brother and sister. They are staying with Uncle John out on his farm".

"It is so nice to meet you," John said.

"It is so nice to meet you too. I have heard a lot about you from Audrey".

To Audrey John said "We were just leaving. Your Mama is pretty tired so don't stay long."

"We won't" said Audrey. "I wanted to give this to Mama. I made it in Bible School" It was a cute little letter holder made from two paper plates and some ribbon with a picture of Jesus and the children.

John looked at it and said "That's great sweetie. I am sure your Mama will be like that".

As Audrey gave the gift to her mother, she said "Uncle John said we should not stay long because you are tired"

"Your Uncle Ed is the boss. Uncle John doesn't know how tired I am. But I am pretty tired. He was right about that. I am so glad you stopped though."

"Tell me" said Mama "How are you and Mrs. Pearl getting along? Are you being a good girl?"

"Mama, I am trying to be as good as I can. I try not to cry over nothing. That makes Aunt Mabel so mad. I don't want Mrs. Pearl to get mad at me too".

Both Mama and Mrs. Pearl laughed. "You do tend to cry a lot over nothing sometimes" said Mama. "It really does upset adults when you cry over nothing. I am glad you are trying to stop that".

"It makes Aunt Mabel slam the door" said Audrey.

Both adults laughed again.

"We will be running along now" said Mrs. Pearl. "Robert said he will take us for ice cream when he gets home this evening. And we have some sparklers we are going to set off after it gets dark. "

"Have fun" said Alice.

Melva thought to herself, "This little girl has brought my husband back to life. I must remember after she is gone to keep a child close. I will just have Jimmy and Jessie over more often after she goes back to her parents".

Harry spent as much time with Alice as he could. He tried to help Mabel with the therapy, but Alice had no patience with him at all. It seemed like she had a little more patience with Mabel, but not much. He felt that he needed to divide himself between Alice and the kids. He tried to see each of the children at least a couple of times a week. They came to visit their mother about once a week, when Ed would allow it. The therapy took most of the day nearly every day now. The children were not allowed to be there during therapy. Alice was usually in pain and she did not want them to see her when she was in such an agitated state. It would not have been good for any of them.

It felt to Alice that she had been here in this bed for years. It had been nearly seven months. She was improving every day, but it was such a little improvement that she felt she was at a standstill. Ed had said that she had made miraculous progress, but she felt that she would never get well. There were still blisters that were infected; Mabel still had to wash the green liquid out every day with the sterile water.

How long could it take? Some days she was so depressed she still wanted to die. Then she remembered that her family was scattered over two states. Some days she thought "If I had died, Harry could be getting on with his life". Then she would remember her children and she knew. "If I had died, Harry would have never been able to get my family back together again".

She was so confused she felt that she was losing her mind. Mabel, who had been her best friend for years, sometimes seemed like a mean and hateful stranger. Mabel pushed her almost beyond her limits. Sometimes she just gave up, and screamed, "No, leave me alone. I can't do this any more". And dear sweet Mabel would walk out of the room. In twenty minutes or so, she would return with that smile like the morning sunshine, and say, "Okay let's try this again".

One minute Alice loved her, the next minute she hated her. But Mabel was always Mabel. She knew that it was just plain torture for Alice, but she also knew it was necessary torture. She could stand it if Alice could. As Alice improved she also became more difficult to treat. Her temper came back with a vengeance. Alice always had a temper, and sometimes it seemed that it was a plus for her. When she felt she couldn't go on, she got so angry, that she managed to find extra strength... The hardest part was learning to move those muscles. The new skin was too tight, it had to give a little, but it just wouldn't give at all. As Alice got just a little more strength, Mabel tried warm wet towels. She would wrap one of Alice's arms in a towel which she had dipped in warm sterile water. Mabel would leave the towel on for a few minutes, and then she would gently try to help Alice to move the joints in her arm. It seemed after a week of this treatment the skin became more bendable.

"I think we're onto something here" said Mabel. Then they started a new regimen. Each day, three times a day, Mabel would help Alice to move, by using this damp cloth method. Mabel seemed to have endless patience. Alice had almost none. As Alice improved Mabel took more time each session, warming towels wrapping Alice in the towels and then helping her to move. It was an endless chore. After about a month of this treatment Alice began to feel that maybe her skin would fit her after all. "Mabel" Alice said one day, "you must have the patience of Job. I have been so mean to you sometimes, but you still come back for more. You should have thrown me out of your house, and even out of your life, but you are still my best friend. How will I ever be able to thank you for all you are doing for me?"

"That's what friends are for" said Mabel. "I know you have been through much more than you put me through. You had no control over what was happening to you. But I knew I did have a little control, I just had to prove it to you. We do what we have to do sometimes, even if it hurts the ones we love".

Chapter 21

Day after weary day these two women worked together. Each day they began to see a little more improvement. Alice could sit in a chair for a little bit longer. Her back, and especially her bottom and the back of her legs, was so tender, that sitting was painful. But the blisters were healing. She began to feel better each day. Now the bandages were being removed a little more each day. It felt good just to know that soon she would be able to sleep on her side. She had been on her stomach for nearly seven months, except for a few minutes at a time when Mabel would force her to sit. At first it had been agonizing. But now she could manage the pain for longer periods. Some days she almost felt like her old self again.

There were still times when she wanted to give up. But they were growing farther apart. She and Mabel were able to carry on conversations as they worked. Alice was able to talk more about the children without crying. Even though she knew they were being very well taken care of, it had been impossible for her to talk about them without feeling that somehow she was neglecting them.

It was about time for school to start again, and three of the girls would be in school this year. Alice felt guilty because strangers, or at the very most, casual friends, were getting her children ready to go back to school. This would be Jean's first year, and her mother could not even go to the school to sign her up. Alice was beginning to take a few steps at a time. As her skin grew to fit her body, she began to get more use of her muscles. She was really on the road to recovery, and it felt so good. But she still was not able to do anything for her children.

Mrs. Pearl brought Audrey in to see her mother one day in mid August. She had a couple of new dresses, mittens and a winter coat with shoes and boots. She also had pencils, paper and crayons in a nice pencil box. Alice cried. It was the first dress Audrey had ever had which her mother had not made for her, and it had to be bought by strangers.

"Alice, please don't feel bad about this. I haven't had so much fun for years" Don't spoil my fun. Even Robert got in on the act. He took her to the shoe store and let her help pick out her shoes. Oh! Alice, it has been such a blessing for us to do this. I hope you don't resent us for it".

"Oh! No" said Alice "I don't resent it, but I do feel guilty. You should not have to do this. You have been so good to her, and taken such good care of her, but you should not have to spend your money on school clothes"

"That was the most fun" she said. "We would have bought more, but we didn't want the others to feel jealous. I know how it is in a big family. It always made me mad if I thought my brother had more than I did, no matter what it was".

"Mama, can I try on the dresses, I would like for you to see me in them. I am so pretty with my new dresses on". Audrey said.

"Sure, Honey" said her mother." I know you are pretty in them. But go ahead if you want to try them on for me"

Audrey tried on one dress and then the other. Each time she turned around and curtseyed. She was so proud. Alice was glad to see her little girl so happy. She was also very glad that this year she would have nice warm clothes to wear to school, where ever that was. She and Harry were still trying to decide if they should uproot the family and leave these dear friends to go to a strange place to find work. This had been on her mind for some time now. They needed to decide soon. It was another big decision they had to make.

Chapter 22

When Harry came in that evening after work he told Alice that he would not need to go back out to the house to work. Joe had found a new caretaker. He said that he was going to go out this weekend, and pack up everything and bring it back to Mabel's. They would store it in the barn for a while until they could make a decision as to where they would go next.

Mr. and Mrs. Friend came in with Jean. She also had some new clothes. "I will pay you back for this" Harry said. "I can't pay it all at once, but I will give you some each month until it is all paid. I did not expect you to do this".

"Oh! No you won't" said Mr. Friend. "Jean has worked for these things".

"Yes" said Mrs. Friend. "We had a deal. She makes her bed every morning, and keeps her room neat. She also helps me to set the table every evening, and washes the dishes, and I dry them and put them away. We have a nice little thing going at our house"

"Yes Daddy I worked hard. I have been a good girl just like I promised you. Look at my pretty new dresses" She held each dress up in front of her, and posed. The adults all smiled. "You really did not have to do all this. But I thank you from the bottom of my heart" said Alice.

"Look Mama" I have pretty hair ribbons to match my dresses, and socks too".

"Yes dear, you will look like a regular princess"

"We have to go now", said Mrs. Friend. "It will soon be time for Jean to go to bed, but she wanted to show her Mama her new things"

Alice started crying again. "Are you sure you won't let us pay for these things. We feel like we are imposing on good friends".

"Don't even think about it" said Mr. Friend. "You will never know how much we have enjoyed these last few months. We sure are going to miss this little one when your family gets back to normal, but we do hope it is soon".

"Take care of yourself Alice, and don't worry about your kids. I think they are all in very capable hands"

"We know they are" said Alice. "That has been the least of my worries while I was lying here. I don't think I could have done it without all the help from my friends".

"Give your Mama a hug Jean, we must go now, but we will come back to visit soon."

Jean hugged her mother, and said "I love you Mama" Then she climbed on her Daddy's lap and kissed him and said "I love you too Daddy. Goodnight".

After they left Harry said to Alice "I feel so bad that other people are buying school clothes for our kids, but they really seem to be genuinely enjoying it. I think maybe our children are regular little good will ambassadors."

Alice laughed. "I think you may be right"

"Now all we have to do is find some clothes for Irene. I know Dad and Mom can't spend that kind of money. I will take her this weekend and buy her some things. I would ask Mabel to come with me, but I think she would insist on paying for at least part of them, and I don't think that would be fair. I just won't say anything until we come back. What do you think she needs?"

"She needs two dresses, and socks to match. She is old enough to know about those things. You can let her help pick them out as long as she doesn't go overboard with the price. She also needs some underwear, and a pair of shoes and boots. They must have boots this winter" I would say just give her a couple of dollars send her into the five and ten, and let her get her own underwear. It would embarrass her for you to be with her. Three dollars should be plenty for underwear. The rest you can buy for her. You should be able to buy a dress for about two dollars. But it will cost at least five for a coat. Be sure it is a warm coat. Don't let her go for pretty unless it is both warm and pretty".

"Will you have that much money? We could wait until next payday for the coat and boots if you don't have that much now. She has that light weight coat that she can wear for a month or so". It does feel good to know that you have a few dollars in your pock if we really need something.

"Well, I have been saving a little" Harry said. "With everyone else taking care of the kids I was able to put some back. I will see what I can get for the money I have. I have ten dollars that I have been keeping to take with me if and when I go to Pennsylvania, and I also have My last paycheck which I have not cashed. It is for twenty two dollars. Our girls will feel like rich kids in real store bought clothing".

"If I was able I could save a lot by making them. I feel so helpless though".

"Well don't you feel guilty about anything. You have worked harder these last few months than I ever worked in my life. You deserve the very best for your kids".

True to his word Harry went to his mother's house to pick up Irene on Saturday morning. He took her to the train station and bought a ticket to Oakdale. Irene was ecstatic. She had never been on a train before. She was so proud to walk down the street in Oakdale with her Daddy. She was so nervous. She was shaking all over when they went into the shop to look at the dresses. "Mama said we should not pay more than two dollars for a dress. So if you see something you like, check the price tag first. Mama said you should wear about a size ten. When you find some things you like, you may try them on. There is a little dressing room back there, and the lady will help you if you need help"

To the sales clerk Harry said "Her mother could not come with us. I hope you can help her find two dresses suitable for school".'

"Of course" said the lady. "Do you know what size you need"?

"Mama said about a ten. I would like a yellow dress. Do you think you have a yellow dress that would fit me?"

"Let's see"

Taking Irene to the rack with some bright little dresses, the sales clerk asked "Is your Mother sick? Your daddy said she couldn't be with you today"

"My mother was burned badly a long time ago. She is starting to get better, but she still can't walk very much. Daddy is buying me some clothes for school".

"I'm sorry to hear that. I hope she is well soon."

"She is going to be better soon. I am sure of that" said Irene.

They found a pretty yellow dress, and then Irene saw a blue one she liked and there was also a purple one she thought was very pretty.

"I don't know which I like best" she said"

The sales clerk said "Why don't you try them all on. We will see which ones you and your Daddy like best. Then you can decide"

She took Irene into the dressing room. She tried on the yellow one first. "Oh I like this one, and it fits me so nice"

She came out to show her dad how it looked on her. He said "Do you like that one?"

"Oh! Yes Daddy. It is just what I was looking for."

Then Irene and the clerk went into the dressing room and tried on the purple dress. She came out for her daddy to see it. "Do you like that one?" He asked.

"Yes, but there is one more I want to try on. Maybe I will like that one better"

They went into the dressing room and she tried on the blue one. "Oh! I like this one too" she said. "Mama said I could only have two.

Which should I get?"

The clerk suggested "Let's see which one your Daddy likes the best".

When she showed this dress to her Daddy, the first thing he said was. "Oh that is the color of your eyes. It looks beautiful on you" Irene said "do you really like it best Daddy?"

"Mama said we should buy two dresses that you like. She did not say that I had to like them. I like all three of them. We know that you want the yellow one. I like the blue one because it is the color of your eyes. But I also like the purple one. You must decide which of the two you like best."

"But Daddy, do you think I look nice in the blue one"

"You look nice in both of them dear. But this is supposed to be your decision. You must make the decision soon because we have some more shopping to do".

"I think I will take the blue one".

Irene and the clerk went back to the dressing room and Irene changed back into her old dress. "I think you made the right decision", said the nice lady. "Your Daddy was right, that dress does match your eyes and it looks beautiful on you."

Harry paid for the dresses, and went across the street to the shoe store. Irene saw a pretty little pair of Patent leather shoes with a buckle. She really liked them but the price was five dollars. She could see that some of the other shoes were not that expensive, so she just passed up those shoes and picked out a nice pair of oxfords. They cost two dollars and a half. She really would have liked to have the ones with the buckle, but she knew they cost too much. She was so happy to have two new dresses, that she told herself not to be selfish. He also bought her a pair of boots to fit over the new shoes.

Afterwards Harry counted his money and told Irene that he had fourteen dollars left. They needed to find a coat, some socks and some unmentionables. He gave her three dollars, and told her to go over to the five and ten cent store and ask the clerk for help if she needed it.

She was so glad that her Dad didn't go with her to buy her underwear. She knew Mama must have told him not to embarrass her. She found what she needed. She even found two pairs of socks to add to her purchase, and took back forty cents change to her Dad.

Then her dad took her to another store and bought her a nice coat. He said "Mama said about five dollars. This coat was six dollars and thirty nine cents, but he said it would be nice and warm and it looked really pretty on her, so he bought it anyway.

Now all of his girls were prepared to start school next month in style.

As they rode home that evening on the train Irene said "Daddy, today was a real adventure for me. I had my first train ride. Bought my first brand new clothes, ate a sandwich in a restaurant and got to spend the day with my Dad all by myself. I feel like a big girl now"

"And you are a big girl now" he said. "Your Mama will be proud of us".

"Sweetheart, while I have you to myself, I would like to talk to you like a big girl. Do you remember when I told you that Uncle Paul had gone to Pennsylvania to get work"?

"Yes Daddy, are we going to move there too."

"Your mama and I have been seriously thinking about it. I don't know for sure if I could even get a job there, but if I could, it would mean I would be making more than twice what I have been making now. What I am making now is not nearly enough for our family. If we were paying rent now, we could not afford to live on what I make. You are older than the others and I know that you realize that your Mama and I have been really struggling. I would like to know how you would feel about moving away from here".

"Daddy, I would not like to move away from here at all. We wouldn't see Grandma and Grandpa very often. And Aunt Mabel, we would miss her so much. But I know that you and Mama need to decide to do something, and I am sure that a better job does sound pretty good to you. I know if we move, I will cry, and I know the others

will too, but we have to do what you and Mama think is best"
    "Your aunt Mabel thinks we should just decide, and then tell you kids. I think you deserve to know what we are thinking about. We really don't have much choice as far as I can see".
    "Daddy, I think wherever we are, it will be okay. We just want us to be together as a family again".

Chapter 23

When Harry and Irene got home that evening, they went in to see Alice. Irene showed her mother the clothes they had bought. She was so happy about her new clothes but she had to talk to her mother about this other thing.

. "Mama" she said. "Daddy told me that we might move to Pennsylvania."

"We have been discussing the idea a lot dear" said Alice. "There is no work here for your dad, and if he can get this job, we think we need to do this. I know that you children will not like the idea, but we have to do something. We really can't continue living the way we have for the last few years. Daddy has to find a job with more security."

"What does that mean Mama?"

"Well sweetheart it simply means that Daddy has to find a job where there will be a steady paycheck. He has been just finding odd jobs, so from one week to the next, we are not sure if we will have any money"

"I see. But would this new job mean more security?"

"It should. When Daddy was working on the railroad we had a paycheck coming in each month. We knew pretty much how much money we would have at the end of the month. For these last couple of years, we didn't know for sure if we would have anything. We can't continue to live like that".

"Mama, we are not babies, except for Harry and Mary. I do pretty well at arithmetic. I will be in fifth grade and I hear a lot of stuff. All we want is for you to get better, and for all of us to be back together. We will be happy then. I have heard Aunt Mabel and Grandma talking. I told Daddy that if we have to move I will probably cry, and I am sure the other girls will too. But Mama we will be so glad for us to all be together, that we will learn to live with it".

"I am counting on you to help the other girls to understand. It is going to be hard for all of us. Your Uncle Ed says that it will be another couple of months before I can go. He wants me to build up more strength. It also is a long ride, and I would not be able to sit for that long yet. What we have been thinking is that your Dad will go back with Uncle Paul next week. He will apply for a job, and if he gets the job, he will find us a house. They have company housing, so if he gets a job, there will be a house for us too. Maybe your dad can have everything ready for us by the time we are ready to go. Maybe we can make the move around the holidays, and you girls won't have to miss much school".

"I am so glad that you are growing up. It's so nice to talk to you like a friend as well as a daughter. I know you are only ten, but you have had to grow up very fast these last couple of years".

"I try Mama. When you get better, and we move, I will help you all I can. I will try to be as grown up as I can".

"Don't grow up too fast dear. It seems that I have missed so much of your childhood; I want you to be a child for a little longer".

"Okay Mama. "I will just try to be as good as I can be".

Mabel came in the room and said "It is time for your Mama's therapy now, so you have to scoot".

"Can I help?" said Irene.

"No", said her mother.

"This is one thing we must do alone".

"Ok Mama I will go"

When Harry came in that evening he told his wife that he had moved their furniture into the back of Mabel's garage. He also told her that he had a talk with Irene about the possibility of their moving, and that she seemed to understand."

Alice told him that she too had talked with Irene.

"Our little girl is growing up" said Harry. "You should have seen the way she handled herself today. She told me that she was nervous. But she was really grown up about everything. She looked at prices and was very thrifty. I saw her eying a pair of shoes in Henderson's shoe store. I know she would have liked to have them. I could tell by the look on her face as she looked at them. But she looked at the price, and just walked past them and picked out another pair that was cheaper. I don't think she knew that I noticed, but I did. If I would have had a little more money I would have liked to buy them for her, but they were not very practical anyway. Then I gave her three dollars and sent her into the five and ten to get her underwear like you said. She got underwear, socks and a hair ribbon, and brought me back forty cents. I thought that was pretty good. I did spend a little more for the coat than you said, but this coat looked so nice on her, and I thought she deserved a little extra".

"As long as you didn't spend all of the money you had saved to go to Pennsylvania" said Alice.

"I still have about twelve dollars and I won't need too much. I will help Paul pay for the gas, and all I need is a little to eat for a week or so. Paul is coming in next weekend. Do you think I should go back with him? I hate to leave you, but I know that you are going to be okay. We could not just pick up and move right away anyway. We need to be sure of a job before we can make the final decision. It will take a few weeks for me to get things ready for you and the kids. Paul said I could stay with him for awhile. Jane and the kids are not there yet. Jane wants to wait until Paul gets a couple of paychecks before she and the kids go out there. I think that is best too. The one thing we won't have there is the support we have here. We will miss Mabel and Ed, Mom and Dad and all our friends. But we can't keep relying on them to pull us out of every jam we get in to".

"That is so true" said Alice. "I feel like I will be losing my best friends in the world".

"You are not losing them, but they will not be as close as they are now".

"I hate to see you go; because I will miss you so much, but I think that will be the best thing to do. The sooner we find out about this job, the sooner we can decide what to do"

Harry left the following weekend with his brother. They all cried when they said goodbye. "Good luck with the job" said Mabel.

Harry called a few days later. "I got the job" he said. "You won't believe how much money I will be making. I will be making almost forty dollars a month and we will live in a company house so we will not be paying rent. Alice we can finally get our heads above water. I plan to save as much as I can from now until the holidays. Christmas will be scarce again this year because we will have to use the money to move. But Honey, I am beginning to see a great future for us"

"You sound like a little boy Harry" Alice said. "I am so happy for you. But try not to dream too high. We still have a long way to go"

"I love you" he said. "I love you too" she answered.

The next month seemed to just drag out. They all missed Harry. Alice was becoming stronger every day. She was up and walking a lot during the day. She was able to rest better at night. She no longer had to lie on her stomach all the time.

The first day of school the three little girls stopped on their way to see their Mama. They were so excited about going to school. They wanted Mama to see them all dressed up in store bought clothes. They felt like princesses. They looked like princesses too. Their Mother cried when they walked into her room. She was so proud of them, but she felt so guilty that they were wearing the first store bought clothes they had ever had, and they had been bought by strangers. It broke her heart, but then she thought, "Maybe this is just the boost we need. Maybe this is that light at the end of that tunnel" She decided to humble herself, and accept these gifts with a full heart.

After the girls had gone to school she told Mabel, "They looked so cute. It did my heart good just to see them so happy. I guess I have to swallow my pride and accept these gifts as a friendly gesture. Now I am feeling guilty for another reason."

"What is that" asked Mabel.

"These wonderful people are falling in love with my children, and now I am going to pick them up and move them to another state. It seems so selfish of me to do that".

"Alice, you are not being selfish. You are doing what you believe is the only thing you can do. I know how you must feel, but you can't do this to yourself".

"I know it is foolish. But I feel that way anyway".

The children told all of their friends at school that they would probably soon be moving away. There were mixed emotions. They were sad, but happy too. They were so glad that their mother was almost well, and the family would soon be back together. They were also happy that their Dad finally had a job. But they were sad to know that they would soon be leaving the only friends they had ever known. Also each girl had become emotionally attached to her temporary family. They knew that it would be a very sad day when they had to say goodbye to them. They had never been farther from Elkton than Oakdale. Pennsylvania sounded like another world. They had no idea what lay ahead for them in this strange place.

Mrs. Pearl cried often that next month. She laughed one day and said "Audrey, maybe you will need to start slamming doors. You said that your Aunt Mabel slams doors when you cry over nothing. Now I am doing that too".

"You are not crying over nothing" Audrey said. "You are sad because I will be leaving you. It is sad that I am leaving you. I am sad also, but I am also happy. How can I be so happy and so sad at the same time?"

"Sometimes that is the way life is" said Mrs. Pearl. "I feel that way too. I am really happy for you. But I am sad for me. I will miss my little girl. But I am glad she will be with her family in a great new place. You will write me letters won't you?"

"I sure will. I will tell you all about my new school, and my new friends"

"I'll have Irene to help me write a letter to you. She can write better than I can.

"I am sure you can write well enough to write me a few lines at least once in awhile. And I will write to you too"

"My mama might have to help me read it because I can't read very well yet. But I am learning"

"I know, and soon you will be surprised at how easy it is for you".

One evening when Jean was sitting on Mr. Friend's lap she said "I am going to miss you when we move" and she started to cry.

Mr. friend hugged her and said, "I am going to miss you too. We have fallen in love with you. It is going to be a sad day when you leave us. But Pennsylvania is not really so far away. Maybe you can come and visit us sometimes. And maybe when school is out in the summer, you can spend some time here with us. Your Aunt Mabel is still here, and I'm sure you will be back to visit her occasionally. You can write us letters, and we can write to you".

"But I can't read and write yet". She said.

"Well, you will learn, and until you learn to write, you can draw us a picture and show us what you are doing. You draw really well Your Mama will read our letters to you, and you can draw us a picture".

Alice was getting stronger every day. The bandages had all been removed. She had scars all over her back and down her arms. But she was so thankful to be alive.

Harry came home for Thanksgiving. The children were all so excited to see him. He had a lot to tell them about Westwood where they were to be living. He told them that there were over three hundred kids in the elementary school there. The house in which they would be living was a double house. The family on the other side had four children: A girl about seven years old and three boys who were younger.

"Westwood was a town much larger than Elkton. 'There are a lot of kids in the neighborhood. I saw a lot of them when I went to look at the house" Harry told them. "I'm sure you won't have any trouble making new friends.

Uncle Paul is moving his family to Pennsylvania this weekend. We borrowed Uncle Wilber's truck. I will drive the truck back with their belongings, and Paul will drive his family in the car. In two weeks we will come back and get you kids and your Mama".

The children all cried when he told them that they only had two more weeks to say their goodbyes. He hugged them all and promised that they would come back to visit often.

During the next two weeks there was a lot of hugging and a lot of crying at several houses in Elkton. Everyone had mixed emotions. Alice tried to get outdoors every day and do some walking. She had not been able to do that until recently. It felt so good just to be able to walk down the street. She took this opportunity to say goodbye to old friends. Everyone was so happy to see her moving around so well. It was ten months since her accident, and she had felt like a prisoner for most of that time. It was so nice just to feel the wind on her face.

Melva took Audrey to Oakdale, and bought her two new dresses. "This is spoiling you" she said. "You don't really need these dresses. But I don't care. I love you, and I want you to be dressed pretty in your new school".

"I love you too" said Audrey. "I will miss you so much when we move. But I am so glad my Mama is better.

"Me too"

Finally moving day came. When Harry drove up to Mabel's in the truck Irene was on her grandmother's porch. Se ran down the street and jumped into his arms. "Oh Daddy" I am so glad to see you". I am going to go and tell the other girls that you are here". And off she went up the street. She first knocked on Mrs. Pearl's door. When Mrs. Pearl answered she said "tell Audrey that Daddy is here. He is at Aunt Mabel's now" Then she ran on up the street to The Friend's place.

Jean was out on the porch with Mr. Friend. "Jean" she said. Daddy is here. He is at Aunt Mabel's. I saw him first"

The girls all ran down the street to Aunt Mabel's house. By the time they got there, a whole crowd of people were gathering. It seemed that everyone in town was there. Harry and some other men were packing furniture onto the truck. Several women were in Aunt Mabel's kitchen with all sorts of food. They had planned a going away party for Harry and Alice and their children. There were people all over the place. Everyone was laughing and talking at once. People were hugging each other. Some were laughing some were crying. The girls didn't know what to make of all of this. Ed came home from Lindale. Even Joe and his wife had come from Washington to see them off.

After the men had the truck loaded, they came indoors and Harry said, "What in the world is going on here. Joe what are you doing back in this part of the country?"

"You didn't think I would let you get away without saying goodbye did you?"

"Surely you didn't make that trip just to say goodbye to me" said Harry.

"Not exactly."

Mabel said, "There is food in the dining room, everyone grab a plate and dig in." When we finish eating a couple of these guys have a few words to say.

Irene and Audrey got them a plate and went to sit on the stairs. "What do you suppose this is all about" said Audrey.

"I don't know" but it seems like we are having a party".

"I know that, but is it someone's birthday?"

"I don't think so"

When everyone had finished eating, Mr. Friend got up and said "We want everybody to know how much we have enjoyed having little Jean with us for the past eight or nine months. She has been a real blessing to us".

Mr. Pearl said "we want you all to know we feel the same about

Audrey. I didn't know that someone that small could brighten up a home so much. Melva and I have decided to adopt a child. We thought we needed a baby, and when we couldn't find a baby we gave up. Now we realize that a child is what we wanted all along. Thank you Audrey for helping us to make this decision".

Ed came and stood in the door way. He said "I have been saving my good news for last. I learned yesterday that my article about the unconventional treatment of Alice's burns has been published in the American Medical Journal. I received a nice little check for it. I am giving Alice fifty dollars, because I think she deserves it"

There was a lot of applause from the group.

Harry said "And now, it is my sad duty to tell all of you so long. This is not goodbye. I promise we will not forget any of you, and we will be back as often as we can. May God Bless each and every one of you.

Harry then jumped into the truck, and the rest of his family into Paul's car, and they were off to a new and better life.

HEARTS ON THE MEND
by Floriana Hall

It is a known fact that heart disease is the number one killer of women. Understanding that, Floriana Hall feels that she is fortunate to be alive today since she had no apparent symptoms. A chance remark to her family physician led to four different tests before it was found out her main artery was 100 percent blocked, two others ninety-five percent, and one ninety percent. She knew about her genetic factor, but was told that her heart was fine at every doctor's visit.

Floriana experienced a quadruple heart bypass on September 4, 2003. She felt compelled to write her bizarre story to help mankind.

Paperback, 78 pages
6" x 9"
ISBN 1-4241-2038-1

About the author:

Floriana Hall, born in Pittsburgh, Pa., on October 2, 1927, is a Distinguished Alumna of Cuyahoga Falls High School, class of 1945. She attended Akron University. She and her husband have been married 60 years, have five children, nine grandchildren and two great-grandchildren. She is a member of St. Martha's church in Akron, Ohio. Floriana has written twelve books, nonfiction and poetry. She is the founder and coordinator of *The Poet's Nook*, a group of local poets who meet monthly at Cuyahoga Falls Library.

also available from publishamerica

INSIDE PASSAGE
by Eunice Loecher

Michelle Lawson wins the trip of a lifetime on an Alaskan inside passage cruise. Disaster strikes in Skagway when a tour bus breaks down, leaving Michelle stranded. While struggling with the decision of how to rejoin her ship, Michelle learns Todd Harper has been released from prison. He is a violent stalker who terrorized Michelle the previous year. Returning home to Erie, Pennsylvania, is no longer a safe option.

After finding a job and a place to live for the summer, Michelle believes she's safe. When a newspaper story reveals her location, Todd Harper comes to finish what he started in Erie.

Paperback, 171 pages
5.5" x 8.5"
ISBN 1-60563-732-7

God teaches Michelle to trust and depend on others. Through it all she discovers acceptance, community and the future God has planned for her.

About the author:

Eunice Loecher is an award-winning author of numerous devotionals, essays, and poems. Her novel, *Living Water*, is available through PublishAmerica. You may contact Eunice at crafty2@newnorth.net or visit her website: www.euniceloecher.com.

UNICORNS DON'T WEAR SHOES
by Helen M. Hogan

When Wes Wilson discovers a body in the barn where he boards his Quarter horse, he faces unexpected accusation from the chief deputy. Wes postpones his dreams—ofcompeting with his stallion in cutting horse shows and of dating Cathy McLeod. He helps rescue Mrs. Magers' lost pony from the slaughterhouse. Young Susan screams in horror as foreman Sutherland kills the stable cat's kittens, so Wilson wades in. As principal, he hopes to expand his high school's programs against opposition from his vin-dictive superintendent. With his teacher accused of kid-napping, Wes figures out the hiding place. Meanwhile, he learns the murder victim is not Mexican but Syrian and in the U.S. with two others on the Homeland Security watch list. The terrorists move in for an explosive ending.

Paperback, 413 pages
6" x 9"
ISBN 1-60441-107-4

About the author:

Retired from teaching college English, Helen judges several horse breeds. She loves traveling with her husband of thirty-eight years, Berry Hogan. The couple enjoy sitting in the backyard swing with a glass of wine and playing with their dogs. Helen M. Hogan's published mysteries include Warning Shot and Driven to Win.

also available from publishamerica

DRAWING CONSTELLATIONS
by Jim Hunter

Galen McNeil always considered himself immune to superstitions…except for this Friday the 13th. One year ago exactly, his girlfriend broke up with him because she claimed God told her to, and Galen can't help but reminisce. His reflections are compounded when an evangelist reads Galen the same passage from the Bible that his ex quoted a year ago that day! The coincidences are almost too much for him when the conversation is interrupted by a beautiful woman who vies for Galen's attention. Stunned by the conflation of past and present, Galen is unable to act and the woman leaves without giving her name or number. For the next week Galen puts up signs in the middle of the park, entreating the woman's return as he tries desperately to regain what was lost and answer tough questions about his life and his place in the world.

Paperback, 151 pages
5.5" x 8.5"
ISBN 1-4241-7380-9

Filled with fully fleshed characters, staccato, realistic dialogue, an off-beat wit, and a philosophical subtext as poignant as it is heartfelt, *Drawing Constellations* presents a gripping cross-section of our culture and our changing time.

About the author:

Jim Hunter was educated at Miami University, Ohio. He currently lives with his family in Oberlin, Ohio. *Drawing Constellations* is his first novel.

available to all bookstores nationwide.
www.publishamerica.com